"You stunned me in...
expression softens. "I was trying
**to stay in control. I couldn't do this
there."**

"This?"

The brush of his lips is balmy, teasing. His tenderness takes me by surprise as does the moment he takes to lean back and search my eyes. I realize he's seeking my consent.

I can hardly think. "This is..."

"What I've wanted to do all night." His gleaming gaze bores into me—intense and unwavering. "*You're* why my pulse is racing."

I just topple right into his arms. He scoops me close and then his mouth is there again—on mine. And I melt.

It turns out that kissing is the best ever way to neutralize panic. The best way to stay in the moment, to not give a damn about anything else in life—not even imminent death. Kissing is the best ever thing full stop.

USA TODAY bestselling author **Natalie Anderson** writes emotional contemporary romance full of sparkling banter, sizzling heat and uplifting endings—perfect for readers who love to escape with empowered heroines and arrogant alphas who are too sexy for their own good. When she's not writing, you'll find Natalie wrangling her four children, three cats, two goldfish and one dog...and snuggled in a heap on the sofa with her husband at the end of the day. Follow her at natalie-anderson.com.

Books by Natalie Anderson

Harlequin Presents

The Night the King Claimed Her
The Boss's Stolen Bride

Innocent Royal Runaways

Impossible Heir for the King
Back to Claim His Crown

Billion-Dollar Christmas Confessions

Carrying Her Boss's Christmas Baby

Rebels, Brothers, Billionaires

Stranded for One Scandalous Week
Nine Months to Claim Her

Jet-Set Billionaires

Revealing Her Nine-Month Secret

Visit the Author Profile page
at Harlequin.com for more titles.

My One-Night Heir

NATALIE ANDERSON

HARLEQUIN®
PRESENTS™

Recycling programs
for this product may
not exist in your area.

ISBN-13: 978-1-335-59359-7

My One-Night Heir

Copyright © 2024 by Natalie Anderson

Harlequin Enterprises ULC
22 Adelaide St. West, 41st Floor
Toronto, Ontario M5H 4E3, Canada
www.Harlequin.com

Printed in Lithuania

MIX
Paper | Supporting
responsible forestry
FSC® C021394

My One-Night Heir

CHAPTER ONE

Talia

'OH, TALIA, thank heavens you're here!'

Despite my exhaustion I shoot Kiri a massive grin. 'Where do you need me?'

'Everywhere.' The chef looks near tears. 'The servers are so inexperienced they need *training* more than guidance but there isn't time. The fryer won't get to temperature and I can't—'

'Leave the servers with me,' I interrupt. It's clear Kiri's hit peak stressed chef and I need to move. Happily, sorting an imploding kitchen situation is something I've done more nights than I want to remember. If I quickly smooth front of house, Kiri can concentrate on her magical plates. She just needs confidence in me for calm to return.

'There aren't enough glasses for the affogatos.' Kiri continues listing the catastrophes.

'I'll find alternative ones.'

'Yeah, but the coffee machine is misfiring and the primary ordered espresso martinis ten minutes ago even though we're only through the third course and have another two—'

'Affogato *and* espresso martinis?' I interrupt again.

'She requested tiramisu as well.' Kiri growls.

I chuckle. She's a customer after my own heart. Coffee's my one true love and I'm going to need my own caffeine hit to get through the next few hours.

'The hired entertainment is late and has only just got onto the gondola.' Kiri tosses a pan into a sink with more force than necessary. 'Typical.'

It's just over a twenty-minute ride in the suspension car to the exclusive restaurant at the top of the mountain so, what with the diva espresso machine and delayed entertainer, there's a gap in proceedings. I can't entertain, but I can tame a coffee machine.

'I'll stall with the martinis,' I reassure Kiri as she whirls back to another pan, furiously stirring its bubbling contents into smooth submission.

'Did you see the forecast?' Kiri growls, stuck in her doom spiral. 'Some apocalyptic storm is due.'

'Yeah?' I bite back a laugh and resort to my fool-proof trick to distract Kiri. 'Well, it only needs to hold off for another couple of hours, then you'll be back down the mountain being massaged by your unreasonably hot husband.'

Kiri's eyes glaze over and her frantic stirring stops. She snaps out of it in time to catch my amusement. 'I know.' She finally cracks a smile. 'I'm losing it.'

'You're fine. Focus on your food. I'll take care of the extraneous. But not even I can change the weather.'

'You sure?' Kiri chuckles mid-sprint from counter to flaming grill. 'I think you're a goddess.'

I'm not. But I *am* used to working back-to-back shifts. I've been doing it since I was thirteen and got my first kitchen-hand job. When Romy—owner of the café I work a day shift at—phoned half an hour before closing saying the manager at the gondola restaurant was down with flu and they desperately needed a head waiter, I said yes. Sure I've already worked a twelve-hour day, plus I have a midnight-till-closing shift at a dive bar later tonight, but I need the money. And not just because of the cost of living here.

Queenstown is mega-expensive. The snowy mountain paradise in New Zealand's South Island is stunningly beautiful with incredible views and adventurous opportunities. It's super popular with the wealthy—there are vast numbers of stunning, luxury leisure homes everywhere. It feels as though every other café customer is a billionaire. They dress in sleek merino jumpers, rock-star jeans and mingle with the travellers who flit in to enjoy the slopes and adrenalin hits. They *all* have high expectations of service. Because I'm reliable I've got more work than I can manage. I hold down multiple food service jobs while building a social media side hustle because, not only do I need to make enough for my own survival, but I support my sister. Ava's four years younger than me and a genius but even with her scholarships she needs additional support, and I don't want our screwed-up family stopping her from succeeding.

So I quickly head out to scope the situation. Honestly, it's pretty wild. Primary guest Simone Boras is Australian, as are her mostly female guests, and for her seventy-seventh birthday she's booked out the entire restaurant. They're loud, they're laughing, they're definitely here to have a good time and we're going to need that entertainment soon to keep the energy up and divert attention from the delay on dessert.

'Simone, I'm Talia.' I smile at her. 'I'm here to make your martinis.'

Simone's polite and charming enough but I recognise the slight edge in her smile. She expects the best. If I deliver, she'll approve. So I move fast. It doesn't take me long to get to grips with the coffee machine and I make her martini. No one makes a meaner coffee than me.

And her delight is genuine. 'Thank you, Talia.'

I don't mind guests with high standards when they appreciate my work.

'Can we get two more of those?' one guest calls to me. 'They look amazing.'

'Of course.' I smile. 'I'll bring them right over.'

As I make more martinis I talk strategy with the servers and send them out with the cocktails. The vibe of the room lifts. When I get a chance I check on Kiri. She's still sweating bullets but the kitchen feels less chaotic.

Pleased, I take a breath and roll my shoulders. While I'd managed a swift shower, put on a clean dress, redone my hair and minimal make-up, my freshen up was only superficial. I'd kill to put my feet up. Instead I head to the storeroom to find those extra glasses. Hopefully a few moments' respite from the noise will help. The view from the floor-to-ceiling windows on the way certainly does. The sun is just setting. Wild clouds skitter over the wide sky, threatening to cloak the mountains in a moody shroud. Below, the city lights twinkle obliviously and the lake stretches into the distance. Some time I'll actually have a day off. I'll not stand for hours, not wait on others. I'll curl in front of a cosy fire and a big window, drink something hot and sweet and do *nothing* but gaze at the view. I'll just *breathe*.

But right now breathing is the *only* thing on that list that I can accomplish. I go into the storeroom, lean back against the door to close it and—

Breathing stops. Jaw drops. Brain…brain…?

Tall. Muscular. Shoulders. Ruffled hair. Rippled abs. Blue eyes. Intense blue eyes. Very intense.

In a succession of still shots, details imprint on my mind one at a time. Matching the frantic beat of my heart.

I know about the abs because he's half naked. He's a chiselled, X-rated, total wow of a man. And he's half naked.

He has a crisp white shirt in his hand and apparently does not give a thought about his state of undress and my observation of it. As I stare he shakes out the shirt and shrugs it up over those broad shoulders. I realise my mouth's ajar but it's dry and I don't shut it. I can't. I can't do *anything* because my brain is completely incompetent. The visuals are more than it can handle. He leisurely begins buttoning the shirt, his abs and pecs and other muscles ripple. He's honestly like not from this earth. And that's when it dawns on me.

'*You're* the entertainment...' I slowly mutter. And yes, I'm marvelling.

Wow. Good for Simone. I really want to be her when I grow up.

His long fingers pause on the third button down. His eyes widen.

'You're late,' I add after an uncomfortable beat. 'It's okay though. They're not even onto dessert yet. They're too busy talking but you're going to stun them into silence.'

There's silence right here, right now. And it only grows.

He's frozen—the half-buttoned shirt still reveals a wide expanse of muscled body. I feel my face getting hotter.

'Is there a problem?' I blink and the smallest portion of brain comes back online. I'm used to sorting problems. 'Do you need help or something?'

'I had to sponge a mark off my shirt.'

'Where?' I squint. It looks perfect to me.

'Here.'

I have to step closer to spot the small smudge.

'Oh, they're never going to notice *that*,' I scoff. 'You should've made it more wet,' I joke. 'That would be...'

At his jerky movement I trail off and clear my throat awkwardly.

'Would be...?' He prompts me.

I glance up and am ensnared in his gaze. He's insanely good-looking. But of course he is. Simone is the type to have only the best money can buy. He must command squillions per performance.

'I thought you guys had like special tear-away shirts and things,' I mumble inanely, trying to turn away but only half succeeding. His isn't some cheap satin suit with easy-open Velcro sides or anything. It's high end. 'Those shirt buttons are stiff. Is it a deliberate thing? To prolong the tease?'

'The tease?' A strange tenor flecks his low echo as he resumes fastening the buttons.

I suppress the shiver skittering down my spine. 'That's what it's all about, right?' I can't stop myself babbling. 'Taking the time, building the anticipation...'

Shut up, Talia.

'Mmm...' He nods and reaches for a black jacket I hadn't even noticed slung on a nearby shelf and pulls a strip of black silk from the pocket. There's a gleam in his eyes that makes shivers ripple through me. 'Could you help me with my tie?'

I don't believe for a second that he can't tie his own bow tie. He'll be taking it off and on multiple times a night.

'I can't do it without a mirror,' he adds, apparently having just read my mind.

I summon self-control. Because I fix things. I oblige. It's what I do. 'Of course.'

I step closer and take the silk. He is much taller than me and I have to rise on tiptoe. Freshly shaven, his jaw is sharp and smooth and I smell a hint of cinnamon. His eyes are very blue and, honestly, I forget what I'm meant to be doing. I wobble. Instantly he puts a hand on my waist to steady me but the contact hits like an electrical current and it resets my heart. It beats faster. I breathe faster too. And my skin seems to have tripled in sensitivity because I *swear* I can feel the heat of him through my dress. Now my legs are wobblier still and suddenly it's not just his hand at my waist, but his arm curled around my back pulling me closer until I'm all but leaning against him. It's *super* embarrassing but there's a glint in his eye that makes me refuse to step back and admit my mortification.

I'm all thumbs. I make myself remember what I'm supposed to be doing. *Simone*. The birthday guest should have the best night of her life.

'They're pretty noisy but in good spirits,' I babble as I tie the silk. 'Mostly women. It's a birthday, you know?'

'I know.'

Yeah, of course he does. He's an absolute professional. He has a calm, confident deliberation about him, there's no rushing him. I can't resist breathing in again to appreciate that cinnamon. His hair has an ever so slightly damp look to it. He's a pillar of sensual heat and I've basically plastered myself all over him.

I'm jealous of Simone and her party. Would it be okay to loiter at the back of the room during his show?

A wave of lust washes over me. I almost choke. I don't behave like this. I don't gawp at men. I prefer to avoid them—I have other priorities. Besides, I don't want to risk discovering I've inherited my mother's appalling taste in men. But I can't stop staring—or *leaning* on him. I even pat his chest once I've finally finished the tie.

'You'll give her a good time, won't you?' I mumble. 'She's nice.'

He blinks. 'A good time?'

My fingers seem to be stuck to his chest. I can't lift them away from the heat of him. The hard strength is compelling. Instinctively I spread them wider. He tenses even more. We're so close and it's madness. I manage to lower my gaze from his but I only get as far as his mouth.

'Do I pass inspection?' he mutters.

'I guess…' I bite my lip.

'Aren't you in charge around here?'

I shake my head. I'm not in charge of anything right this second and that is so not like me. 'I'd better get back to…'

'To what?' He leans a little closer.

I manage to breathe but I get another hit of that soap and I'm brainless again. 'Making coffee. I make a lot of coffee. But that's okay. I actually love making coffee.'

He nods. 'I love my job too.'

Yeah. 'I bet you're really good at it.'

'So I've been told,' he says gravely.

I should step back but he hasn't released me and I'm completely immobilised. There's another long moment where we stand too still, too silent, too close. My heart is pounding so hard he must be able to feel it. His mouth moves and he actually smiles. Everything seems awfully intimate but at the same time it's shockingly *easy*. I don't know this feeling. It's as if I've stepped through a portal and now a swirling bubble of heat spreads from a secret source low in my belly. Warmth and light ripple through me, and something silkier—something forbidden. It snakes around me like a ribbon, drawing me closer. Binding me to him. I don't want it to end.

I hear something like a groan and with a small gasp I realise it came from *me*.

I'm too busy. I'm too alone. But I need to be. Ava is relying on me. Romy is relying on me. Kiri is relying on me. So is Simone. And *I'm* relying on me. There's no one else I *can* rely on.

'You really shouldn't be any later,' I say firmly.

'You really care about whether she has a good time?'

'Yes,' I growl. 'I really do. And not because she's paid for it. She's a nice person. How people like her treat people like me and you is very telling.'

'People like her?'

'Obscenely wealthy.' Aside from the whole book-the-whole-restaurant-out fact, Simone has the look—the silk clothes and gleaming jewels. Most of the ultra-wealthy people I've met are too used to getting whatever they want. At best they take people like me for granted and at worst, treat me like dirt. Either way I know very well I don't fit in their world. 'But she's a good one.'

His expression tightens. 'To people like you and me?'

'Service industry survivors.' I half smile. Bracketing myself with him feels good. 'She deserves a good night,' I say softly. 'Don't make her wait any longer.'

'Okay,' he agrees equally softly but he doesn't release me. 'I won't make her wait…'

I'm struck by the craziest thought that he's about to kiss me. The even crazier thing is that I'm about to let him.

'Talia?' Kiri's voice pierces through the door. 'Any luck?'

I flinch, returning to reality with a jump. He steps back. Cold air ripples over the space on my back where his arm rested. I brace to stop myself stumbling after him.

Kiri's question slowly sinks in. I've completely forgotten why I came in here and I have no idea how long I've been standing here just—

'Glasses,' I remember dazedly. 'I need to find glasses.'

'That's why you needed to get so close just now?' A low laugh escapes him. 'So you could see me properly?'

'See your tie. Yes.' But I can only stare at him again—his smile steals everything.

'Sorry, sweetness. No luck tonight.' He leans forward and kisses me on the cheekbone. It's such a soft, swift brush of his lips that I wonder if I imagine it.

I don't answer. I can't. My brain is mush.

CHAPTER TWO

Dain

I CAN'T REMEMBER who I am or why I'm here or what I'm supposed to be doing. All I know is a scrap of a waitress urged me to do a 'good job' and all I want is to please *her* in every carnal way imaginable. *That* urge was so overwhelming I just kissed her cheek and a bolt of electricity slammed into me. Fortunately my reason returned with the force of it. Even so I stare at her for a second longer. She has shockingly pretty, big brown eyes—like a deer. She's a bit of a Bambi all round with her slim, leggy build and her glossy black-coffee hair. Pretty thing materialised just as I'd sorted the ink stain on my shirt and helped me dress like some over-efficient boarding-house matron with nimble fingers and sweet concentration. Most women undress me. This one helped me do the opposite and it was one of the hottest moments of my life. Go figure.

Talia. It's a delicate name for a delicate creature and I've a craving to taste more than just her name. Sex is a private pleasure I don't take too seriously but I must admit that being mistaken for a stripper is a first. I'll strip if she wants—*her*, that is—out of that black dress. I want to do more than strip her. I want to hear her moan again. I want her to melt against me.

It's instant and it's *intense*.

But given I haven't indulged recently, maybe it's reasonable that desire bites so hard now. My work-life balance has been more out of whack than usual. But *she's* at work and I can't harass her. Plus she's even more confused as to who I am and why I'm here than I am. Right now I'm too amused and bemused to tell her. And, all right, yes, aroused. So I walk out of the room and down the corridor. There's a ripple as I walk into the restaurant. I glance behind me, stupidly vain enough to hope she sees the reaction to my arrival. But she hasn't followed me. Deflated, I stroll towards Simone, seated in the centre of the party. The woman beside her moves to make room for me.

'You were supposed to be here hours ago,' Simone admonishes as we hug. 'But I don't mind.'

Some people write Simone off as an airhead—a Sydney society eccentric. They're wrong. She has an astute business brain. She's also the only person from my past with whom I retain consistent contact outside the boardroom.

'I'm glad you made it,' she adds.

So am I, though not for any reason to do with my godmother. I'm haunted by the sound of a sexy little inhale as I brushed that completely inappropriate kiss on Talia's cheek.

'What held you up?' Simone asks.

I'm not about to offer full disclosure. 'Meeting ran overtime. You forgive me, right?'

Simone smiles. 'If you invest in this project, you know I'll forgive you anything.'

My smile becomes a little fixed. Even though she's almost family, Simone still wants my money. Like everyone. 'You know I can't give you an answer on that without seeing the paperwork.'

She sighs dramatically. 'Must you be so vigilant, Dain?'

'Always.'

Business comes first but I do owe Simone and that's why I'm here.

My family's been in the residential property development business for decades. My great-great-grandfather founded the business and built it to a high level of success that was subsequently almost entirely destroyed by the viciousness of my parents' divorce. They tore the company apart as well as their marriage. As well as me.

But it was down to me to resurrect what I could from the wreckage of it all. Because of Simone I was able to fulfil the promise I'd made to my grandfather. And I've done it. Anzelotti is the largest luxury apartment building company in Australia. We build thousands of them each year and still can't satisfy the waiting list.

Expansion into New Zealand hasn't been a priority, but Simone's been making a case for my investment here for the past two years. Having her birthday party tonight was in part a deliberate act to entice me back to Queenstown. I was happy to indulge her but now I'm distracted because Talia appears in the room. Yeah, she *is* the one in charge. She's ultra-efficient—minimal actions, maximum impact— and happily she's aware of me. It's barely two beats before she spots me sitting next to Simone. Her face is a picture before she pulls on a professional mask. She approaches immediately. Not going to lie, I'm delighted.

'Is everything to your satisfaction, Simone?' she asks.

She doesn't look at me as Simone answers in the affirmative.

I can't resist teasing her. 'I heard something about the entertainment having arrived?' I cock my head. 'Or is it running late?'

A flush sweeps her cheeks and she flashes a baleful look my way. 'I'll find out and get back to you as soon as I can.'

I can't help but chuckle. Then I count the seconds until she returns.

'It'll be just another few minutes and then the singer will be here,' she says.

'Singer?' I clarify coolly. 'Not a dancer?'

'No.' Her teeth snap as she smiles sharply.

'I'm going to need more coffee to keep me awake for the performance,' Simone says, seemingly oblivious to the undercurrents between the waitress and me. 'Any chance of a latte?'

'Of course,' Talia says. 'I'll get that right away.'

I can't remain still for more than a few moments. 'Excuse me, Simone,' I mutter.

Talia stands by the coffee machine. As I approach I have to suppress the maddening urge to run my hand the length of her stiff spine and soften her curves against me again. I take a sharp breath instead. Public flirting is not my thing and I definitely don't touch a woman in view of anyone else—I don't even hold hands. Discretion is everything to me. My personal life is and always will be utterly private. So that I'm openly obvious with my attention is a first. Women are usually obvious with me. All I need do is discreetly nod and they approach. From there it's to my private suite. I know that sounds arrogant but it's just true. It's what happens when you're one of Australia's wealthiest bachelors. Only I'm not in Australia now and this woman avoids my gaze entirely. But I know she's aware of me. There's strong chemistry between us and we both know it.

'I'm really looking forward to the singer,' I say conversationally.

Her body goes tense.

'Or is there some problem?' I add. 'Perhaps you'll have to step in and fill the breach?'

She ducks her chin and her flush deepens. I actually feel a little bad for teasing her.

'You should have told me you were her date,' she mutters meekly.

I blink. She thinks I'm Simone's *date*? Good grief, I've gone from stripper to escort. She glances up and that's when I spot the gleaming tease in her eyes. It tugs deep in my gut—it makes me want to use some sort of *physical* correction with her.

'Simone Boras is my godmother,' I inform her as coolly as I can. 'She's the nearest thing to a grandmother I have.'

Talia's expression flickers with smug amusement before she smooths it. I narrow my gaze on her.

'So I'm not about to give her or any other woman here a lap dance.' I lean close. 'Though I'd make an exception for you.'

That colour deepens her skin but I'm struck by the molten emotion in her bottomless eyes. I shouldn't have said it. I'm like some lecherous party guest. But she provoked me and we had shared a moment in that storeroom. Now she presses her trembling lips together—not pursing them in disapproval, but suppressing her smile. That ache tugs deep inside me again and I want everyone in this room to vanish so we can be alone.

'Can I please get a coffee too?' I mutter. 'Black. No sugar.'

'Of course.' She swiftly operates the machine.

Even though I never do this—I never usually *have* to—I somehow end up telling her who I am. 'My name is Dain Anzelotti.'

Her expression is back to bland. 'Am I supposed to recognise your name?'

'Many people would.' My name is on a lot of contracts.

But I'm not surprised she didn't recognise my face. I avoid all kinds of media. I can get some stories scrubbed before they hit the mainstream press and I only attend social events where discretion is assured. I'm not on any social media platforms. I don't have a personal email address. When you're as wealthy as I am it's advisable to remain as unreachable as possible. So as far as I'm aware there are no social media pictures of me anywhere now and, yes, I'm too precious but I've had more than enough of those in my past when I was used as a pawn during my parents' drawn-out separation and brutally public divorce.

She looks down at the coffee cup she's filling. 'You're not local, right?'

'Right. But…' But most people recognise my name.

'Are you famous or something?'

'Or something.'

'By that you mean wealthy.' She shoots me a cutting glance. 'So what? In Queenstown every other customer is an arrogant billionaire. Which sort are you? Tech? Rural? Some sort of amazing eco-friendly attire?' Her gaze rakes over my suit. 'Snowboard champion?'

'Property development,' I mutter.

She doesn't look impressed. 'Hotels?'

'Apartments.' I don't know why I'm suddenly like a schoolboy struggling to impress the girl he fancies on the bus.

'Good for you.' She shrugs dismissively.

'You'd prefer I was an…entertainer?'

She pauses. 'Well…' Her voice drops. 'It does seem like a waste of your other assets.'

I'm so shocked I can only stare as that husky little sass repeats in my head. Desire paralyses me. The images in my head—how I could use the 'assets' she's thinking of—are shockingly inappropriate. I don't lose control of myself like this. Definitely not in public. I blink, needing to distract myself before this very crowded room sees the effect this woman has on me. My gaze drops and I see the latte she's made for Simone. I've seen fancy patterns on top of frothy milk before, but this one is particularly artistic with a highly detailed bird hovering over a flower.

'That's amazing,' I mutter hoarsely.

'Yes.' She glances up and looks me directly in the eyes. 'Tastes even better.'

I'm gone. Brain dead. Body slammed. Stunned into silence. I don't respond at all. Where did this vixen come from? I've been hit on more times than I can remember but this tiny attempt has me sizzling in a way I can't handle. I recall the moments in that storeroom where she was pressed against me. I want that again. I'm all but overpowered by the urge to toss her over my shoulder and carry her back there to finish what we started.

But I don't. I can't. I remain still and silent. Struggling to process, to regain control of myself. It takes too long. Belatedly I realise a flush has swept over her face. Before I can think to respond or am able to un-gum my mouth, she drops her gaze. Swiftly she sets the coffees on a small tray. Distractedly I notice other differences between my small, plain drink and Simone's.

'Don't I get a cookie too?' I ask feebly.

It's too late. She doesn't answer. She doesn't look me in the eyes. Since when was I so incompetent with a woman? I follow her like a redundant fool. She's mortified. Even the tips of her ears are scarlet. I slip back into my seat.

'Have you been giving her a hard time?' Simone asks quietly as I watch Talia march back across the room—stiff-backed, scarlet-cheeked.

Not the kind of hard time I want to give her, no.

'She's not your usual type,' Simone adds speculatively.

'Surely you don't think I have a singular type.' I sip my scalding coffee to hide the frustration overflowing within me but I can't lift my attention from Talia.

Simone's tone warms with exasperated amusement. 'Aren't you ever going to settle down?'

'Surely you don't need to ask that.'

Because it was Simone who pulled up to my boarding school and helped me escape one of the worst moments of my life—the media intrusion and the shock of secrets kept from me until it was too late. She knows how I was caught in the midst of an emotional massacre and that I'll never accept the blistering bonds of a committed relationship myself.

'No,' Simone acknowledges. 'But you're never obvious in public. This is intriguing.'

But I haven't felt temptation like this. Or such uncertainty. I don't usually have to work for it.

I tear my gaze from Talia to focus on Simone—she's the reason I'm here, after all, and Talia was right, Simone is one of the good ones. 'I'm sorry. It's your birthday.' I pull a small box from my pocket and put it on the table between us.

Simone all but shimmers. 'Is it a pen to sign the investment papers?'

I laugh at her persistence. 'You know any deal will be negotiated in the office.'

But I remind her gently because Simone tried to help me all those years ago. A close friend of my grandfather, she disapproved of him keeping secrets from me. And she was the only one to take action when the press found out he was terminal.

'I promise I'll look at it properly tomorrow,' I add with a smile. 'I'll be there at nine.'

I enjoy the coffee and the dessert and talk to Simone and several of her guests. I also enjoy watching Talia care for the guests. That she's determined not to look in my direction is actually reassuring. She's as aware of me as I am of her and I just need another moment with her. Alone.

A guy with a guitar arrives. The long-haired crooner sings hits of bygone years. Simone loves it. But partway through his fourth item I sense an emptiness in the room. It's only been a few moments but I'm acutely aware Talia's gone. I mutter something to Simone and move.

I catch up with a young waiter in the corridor. 'Where's Talia?'

The young man looks both startled and awkward. 'She's just finished for the evening.'

Disappointment floods me. 'She's not staying till closing?'

The youth fidgets. 'She was only helping out for a while before she had to—' He stops before saying anything truly useful. 'Is there something I can get for you, sir?'

'No, that's fine. Thank you.'

I message Simone to apologise for my sudden departure and confirm tomorrow's meeting time. I know she won't mind—I've stayed longer than she'd have expected me to anyway. Striding towards the gondola, I notice the sky has darkened. The wind's lifted, whistling around the outside of the building. There's only one way down from this place and this is one ride I refuse to miss.

CHAPTER THREE

Talia

IN THE SMALL crew room I scoop up my small backpack, shove my apron into it and hurry down the corridor. I can't get out of here quick enough. I've made a massive fool of myself trying to flirt with that guy. He's more than a guest of the primary, he's her *godson*—practically family. Of *course* he wasn't a stripper, not in a suit that beautifully made and fitted and from fabric that soft and flattering. Why did I leap to such an inappropriate conclusion?

Because he was half naked and is so stunningly sculpted it was the only possibility to hit me. Yes, I objectified the guy. And no, I don't usually do that. I've avoided guys my whole life. That's what happens when your 'charming' father's a serial cheater and your co-dependent mother's a serial sucker—falling for the same type over and over. That kind of example puts a girl off even trying.

But Dain Anzelotti could have corrected me sooner, instead he let me make a bigger and bigger fool of myself until at last he revealed his innate arrogance. He flipped from smoothly amused to steely and silent—shooting me down without uttering a word. I was incinerated on the spot. But *he* kissed *me*—the patronising jerk only wanted to hook me in order to feed his endless ego. As if all his supposed wealth wasn't enough to make him feel special? Once I was on the line he couldn't cut me quick enough. I need to get out of here before I stomp back to give the entitled jerk a piece of my mind.

The gondola engineer is engrossed in some sports game onscreen and barely notices me waiting for the small passenger cabin that's coming round on the track. The cabins aren't huge and it's a relief to have it to myself. I've been customer servicing for hours and this is only a respite before I get to the bar down in town and carry on fulfilling people's orders. Still hot and flustered, I toss my backpack onto the seat with too much force. It slips straight off and I groan in frustration as my things scatter everywhere. I slump on the seat. There's no rush to collect everything, I have over twenty minutes to pull it together.

I hear rapid footsteps and hope whoever it is will be polite enough to wait for the next cabin. But a big hand stops my door from sliding shut and the suspension car wobbles as he steps inside. There's a bumping sensation as the cabin moves over the pulley system. I don't love the gondola—being suspended high above the jagged edge of a mountain freaks me out a little. But right now I'm more freaked out about the view *inside* the cabin.

I stare at him in consternation—the entertainment who wasn't. The self-proclaimed billionaire property magnate. He takes the space on the seat beside me, the doors bang shut and then there's silence as he stares at my stuff scattered all over the floor.

'What happened?' he eventually asks. 'Did you have a tantrum?'

Stunned, I do nothing as he slides onto his knees in the small space in front of me. He retrieves the items one by one—my comb and a spare hair tie, headphones that I can't use now to avoid this conversation, coins, my favourite tinted lip balm and some pain relief. He passes each item for me to stuff back into my bag and meets my gaze every time.

It's immensely irritating that he's so handsome. That my body is literally melting. What's with his mixed messages?

'Thanks,' I mumble, embarrassed and confused.

The heated intimacy in his eyes bamboozles me. As much as I want to, I can't look away from him.

'Why are you skipping out early?' Having gathered all my gear, he gets up from the floor and sits beside me. 'Have you got a date?'

I feel myself flushing. 'Another job to get to.'

'You often double shift?'

Determined not to let him get to me more, I lift my chin. 'Triple.'

He doesn't take his gaze off me. 'You need the money.'

'Most of us mere mortals do.'

He nods as if he understands. But he can't possibly. What does he know of struggling daily for survival? Of responsibility? I've been responsible, not just for myself, but for my little sister, Ava, since I was eleven and she was seven. After Dad skipped out and Mum went down a spiral of bad choice after bad choice, I needed to ensure Ava got through school—I had to because she's gifted. Seriously super smart, but having to shift schools so many times when we were kids impacted her despite her insane IQ and the intense extra study she did. So I worked and when Mum wanted to make one move too many I said no. I took on Ava myself age seventeen and I was super happy to. I wanted her to have the stability she needed—that we'd never had.

I still support her now, six years later. And once she's finished her studies, I'll focus on my own future.

'I should have told you I wasn't the entertainment,' he says after a long silence. 'But I was taken by surprise and the temptation to tease you was irresistible.'

'It was my fault for jumping to conclusions,' I say stiffly.

'It seems like you'd prefer I was a booty dancer to a billionaire.' His smile briefly quirks. 'Don't you like me now you know I'm basically made of money?' He actually shoots me kicked-puppy eyes. 'It doesn't usually work that way.'

'Doesn't it?' I murmur shortly, so easily provoked into outrage all over again. 'What? Don't tell me you're some poor little rich boy now seeking my sympathy?'

The curve of his mouth deepens. 'Right now I'll take anything I can.'

I shake my head. 'You've got enough from me already.'

'Oh, I disagree,' he counters softly.

I glare at him but at the same time I'm almost helplessly drawn to him. He's more good-looking than most. Honestly, he's more *everything* than most.

'I'm glad you've finished work early. Now I'm allowed to talk to you,' he adds.

'Allowed?' I echo. 'As if you pay attention to the rules anyone else abides by?'

'You really think you have me nailed, don't you?'

The most appalling flush swamps me. I'm so hot I can't even swallow. It's a replay of that moment in the storeroom when I stood too close to him and he held me against him and time stilled.

An ominous clunking sound breaks the searing spell between us and the cabin sways awkwardly. Startled, I glance out of the window. Usually the view is spectacular when the moon and stars cast a glow over the lake but tonight the celestial elements are obscured by clouds. That clunk is replaced by a sharp metallic screech.

I've no idea how long we've been in the cabin or how far we've descended but I know we have to be some distance from the bottom still. Meaning we're suspended above a rocky mountainside and if the cable breaks we'll smash down and likely won't live. Just then the sky lights up—yet illuminates nothing. The lightning just bounces back from the thick cloud. The storm has hit sooner than predicted.

'I—'

The cabin light flickers before cutting out completely.

'Um…' Dain pulls his phone from his pocket.

As he studies the screen I hear his smothered curse.

'We've lost reception,' he says.

'It doesn't seem like there's power in town,' I mutter, pointlessly peering out of the window.

I hear the wind whistling around us. How did I not hear it pick up so much during the descent? I've been too distracted by *him*. But this is a major problem. We're suspended in a tin can, high above a jagged mountain in a major weather event. My pulse skitters.

'You feeling okay?' His query is soft.

I nod, then realise he can't see me but even in this darkness he's sensed my rising nerves. I don't want to think about how far we could fall. How we'd smash to smithereens. 'Yeah,' I lie. 'Are you?' I squeak.

'I'm hanging in there.'

I smile weakly. 'Tragic attempt at a pun.'

He turns his phone's torch on, sits it between us and smiles at me. It's a gorgeous smile and it humanises him and with him half hidden in the dark he feels more accessible.

'I feel wobbly,' I say. 'Like the ground has vanished beneath my feet.'

My joke is even more feeble but it's better to challenge my brain to come up with puns instead of staying fixated on his attractiveness. But my brain does that anyway. Relentlessly.

There's another sudden jolt and the cabin sways in a way it isn't supposed to. I draw a sharp breath. Dain's phone slides off the seat and lands on the floor, lighting the corner instead of us. He doesn't move to retrieve it. Instead he puts his hand on mine. I'm so unashamedly grateful I twist my fingers to grasp his and cover his wrist with my other hand. Just like that I'm clinging and I don't care.

'It might take some time for them to get power back online,' I worry.

'There isn't a generator?'

'I don't know. I don't usually work up there. I was just helping out a friend.'

'You enjoy your work?' he asks calmly.

'I've been doing it a long time.'

'Your latte art was pretty cool. I've seen some done before but your bird design for Simone was excellent.'

'Thanks.'

'You must have practised a lot.'

I know he's distracting me. I welcome it. I drag in a breath and make myself focus. 'Yeah, but mostly I do it to put online. I have a social media channel for it.'

'You have an influencer side hustle?'

I swear I hear an element of judgement in his tone. 'I'm hardly at influencer status but my ASMR videos are really popular. And my how-to-do-it-at-home tutorials are increasingly getting clicks.'

'And that's the dream—to be an Insta-recognisable influencer?'

Oh, there's definitely judgement there.

'Actually, I'm going to have my own roastery one day. My own coffee label. And my channel is absolutely going to help with that.' I'm not trying to impress him. I'm just babbling. It's helping but not as much as his hand-holding is.

'You want to take on the big multinationals?' he asks.

'No, I just want a boutique label. I want to support coffee growers with ethical practices who provide a sustainable wage. There's room in the market for that and the world needs to change.'

'You're an idealist.'

I shake my head. 'A humanist.'

The light from the phone on the floor in the corner is just enough to let me see him, hopefully without him seeing how much I'm staring. *He's* the perfect distraction from the fear that I'm about to plummet hundreds of feet onto rocks. His eyes are stunning. A deep blue, they glitter with a vitality that makes me want to lean in to feel his energy. Okay, his muscles too. I want to test out the length and breadth of him for myself. It's the weirdest thing. I avoid men. But this isn't like anything else. This is like a lightning strike and, yes, I know that's a cliché, but it's the best my befuddled brain can come up with right now. I guess the storm outside is a prompt and all.

'They should have shut down the gondola,' I murmur. 'We'd be safer up at the top even without power.'

'We'll be fine.' His hand tightens on mine. 'We're more likely to be in a car accident.'

'You know your facts.' Who's he trying to reassure? Me or himself?

'Several.'

'You're a one-per-center, though. You're already in a bunch of minority sections. Top of your class. Most wealthy.'

Most gorgeous.

'And you think that makes me more likely to be killed in a freak gondola accident?' He sounds amused.

'You're all kinds of special,' I mumble.

His hand tightens on mine. 'Look at me,' he says softly. 'We're going to be fine.'

'You don't know that.' But I breathe out slowly. I am not going to lose it here. I never lose it. I stay calm even when a situation seems dire. 'But there's nothing either of us can do in this moment to make it better.'

'No?'

I pause, struck by a sudden frisson in the atmosphere between us.

'Powerless is not a position I'm used to being in,' he says.

I can well believe it. And, even though I mightn't have the money he does, I do have my own drive. 'Me neither.'

'You were in charge of all the wait staff.' He nods. 'You're usually in control?'

'Of everything front of house.'

'Yeah,' he mutters. 'You were more than efficient. You control everything else too. Multiple jobs—even how the milk spills into a cup...'

I loathe feeling as though I have no control over my life. My whole childhood was hostage to my mother's whims. Ava and I had no choice about where we lived or for how long. Mum made us pack up and move on in an afternoon. I left places and people I loved without the chance to say goodbye or explain why. That's not how I live now and it's not how *I'll* ever make anyone live.

'Two control freaks trapped in a stalled gondola in the middle of an electrical storm...what a nightmare.' I manage a smile.

He smiles back. 'It's not so awful.'

I shoot him a sceptical look. 'I can feel your pulse racing.'

'It is,' he says. 'But not because I'm scared.'

My pulse races. Not because I'm scared either. 'I guess there's nothing like a natural disaster as a great leveller. Your money isn't going to make any difference now.'

'Have I lost what little lustre I had?' He's mock mournful.

'You know I was never attracted to your billions, but your brawn could still be useful.'

'Brawn?' He almost chokes on a laugh. 'How so?'

Searing temptation takes hold of me and suddenly it doesn't matter that he froze me out the last time I tried flirting with him. This time he's intimately close—I can feel his pulse, see his smile, and it's intoxicating. 'I think my chances of survival will be higher if you cushion my landing.'

'What?' His jaw drops.

'If you're wrapped around me I'll be protected.'

'So I'll go splat and you'll be saved.' He smiles. 'From this height?'

Amusement shimmers through us both.

'I'm happy to increase my odds even if it's only by an infinitesimal amount,' I breathe.

He leans closer. 'Are you asking me to hold you?'

I can't answer. His grip on my fingers tightens and while he cups my jaw with his other hand he leans closer still. I stop breathing.

And my stomach rumbles. Loudly. I stifle a moan. As if it weren't mortifying enough to be so gauche in here with him.

'You're hungry,' he teases softly.

I'm thirsty too. Frankly I have all kinds of needs right now. 'I'll survive.'

But my pulse skips. If this is the moment before my

death then I don't want to go without having ever kissed a man. And a man is right here with me and he seems like he might—

'Do you need distraction from that as well as the imminent disaster?' he asks.

'What kind of distraction are you thinking of?'

'Well, *you* did think I was the entertainment but I think a lap dance might make the car swing too much. I think we're going to have to take this gently and slowly.'

I stare at him warily, because when it comes down to it I can never trust anyone. 'You froze me out with your silence in the restaurant.'

'No. You stunned me into silence.' His expression softens. 'I was trying to stay in control. I couldn't do this there.'

'This?'

The brush of his lips is balmy, teasing. His tenderness takes me by surprise, as does the moment he takes to lean back and search my eyes. I realise he's seeking my consent.

I can hardly think. 'This is...'

'What I've wanted to do all night.' His gleaming gaze bores into me—intense and unwavering. '*You're* why my pulse is racing.'

I just topple right into his arms. He scoops me close and then his mouth is there again—on mine. And I melt.

It turns out that kissing is the best ever way to neutralise panic. The best way to stay in the moment, to not give a damn about anything else in life—not even imminent death. Kissing is the best ever thing full stop. We kiss and we kiss and we kiss.

I have no idea how long we've been stuck here and I no longer care because there's this and this is the beginning, the end, the everything.

He pulls me onto his lap, wrapping his arms around me.

So tight. So right. I actually quiver and his embrace tightens still more. I'm twisted sideways but I manage to free my arms to wind them around his broad shoulders and we just keep kissing. He's hot and his attention is lush and he carries me with him.

This is nothing but a moment in the middle of a storm. He'll be leaving the country shortly. I'll never see him again. So I'm not just here, I'm all in as a need I've long denied unleashes within me.

'What was it you said?' He growls, picking up on my restless hunger. 'She deserves a good night and I shouldn't make her wait any longer...?'

His hands sweep over me as he plunders my mouth. I shiver even though I'm hot. He palms my breasts then shapes my waist. I feel his tension, the ridge of his arousal beneath me. I moan as I realise he's as hot for me. I want it with him. I want it all. He slips his hand beneath my dress. The trail of his fingertips against my skin makes my moans earthier. I can't retain control of myself. My hips rock to a rhythm that's new to me yet is as old as time. He doesn't stop—he targets his attentions. Because he knows what he's doing. He knows how his touch sends me mad. Dissolving all thought, leaving only feeling. *Need*.

'Sweetheart,' he mutters as he pushes my panties aside. 'All this wet is for me.'

I gasp and groan at the same time—torn between extreme arousal and embarrassment. It's not a pretty noise.

But he gives further encouragement. 'So sweet, I want to taste it.'

Oh. I melt even more because to my astonishment I want that too but there's no time. I'm not anywhere near naked nor is he but it doesn't matter because I start to shake.

'Oh, darling...' His tongue slides past my lips and into

my mouth, invading my heat the way I know he wants to plunder that other part of me.

I ache with searing need. His hand moves more intimately against me and he slides a finger inside my virgin flesh. I gasp—his possession is such a relief but still isn't enough. I rock my hips. Riding him. He holds me firm while stroking me, gruffly purring encouragement.

'I want...' I can't finish my sentence.

'I know what you want.' He growls roughly. 'Come on me, Talia.'

It's so intimate I could die. But he orders me into a raw response with coarse, lusty words that make me hotter, slicker, wilder until at last I convulse. I tear my lips from his to shriek through the unbearable ecstasy.

It's good. Oh, it's good.

I squeeze my fingers into his shoulders as I shudder, gasping for big breaths to recover something of myself. I've just come apart completely. I've never lost control like this with anyone. But in *his* hold, it's not just empowering, it's addictive. Only the totality of that insane satisfaction lasts mere seconds. With a moan I kiss him with complete abandon. Showing him what I can't verbalise—I want *more.*

He groans and his hand cups my sex possessively. 'Talia...'

'Yes.' Unfettered, I pant between kisses. 'Yes, yes, yes.'

His whole body tightens beneath me. 'You want—'

'Yes!' But a sliver of sanity stirs and I lift my head. 'But I can't get pregnant or—'

'Your fellow control freak has a condom in his wallet.' His words are muffled against my neck as he suckles my skin. 'Kids aren't on my agenda.'

He's unapologetic but his obviously vast experience isn't a turn-off. I know nothing. He knows everything. I could learn. I *want* to learn. Especially with him. Here's my chance. I'm not afraid of anything any more. For the first time in my life I'm fearless—such is the power of that orgasm and the madness in this moment.

'Not mine either. Not yet for me.' I glance at him. 'Not ever for you, right?'

'Right.' He chuckles lightly. 'So let me get it.'

He wriggles to dig out his wallet. I just get more aroused all over again.

'Look at us. Capable people. In control,' he mutters.

'So in control.' I'm sliding towards oblivion again—*so* fast.

'Rational right to the end,' he insists with mock seriousness as he teases me even more.

'Stop congratulating yourself on your genius and put it on.'

'Right. Ms Impatience.'

'Of course I'm impatient.' I lean against him. 'We're hanging by a thread and who knows how long we have…?'

He laughs but it morphs into a groan. 'Quite.'

He lifts me to my feet, moving me only slightly away from him, and delves beneath my hemline again to slide my panties down and off. He doesn't bother taking off my dress. There isn't time. He balances me with one hand while hurriedly unfastening his trousers, lifting his hips enough to bare his thighs and free his straining erection. Then he pulls me back onto his lap with strength that awes me. This time I'm fully facing him, my legs straddle him. Even though I'm basically still dressed, I'm more exposed than I've ever been in my life.

He kisses me, unfastening the first few buttons of my dress with deft skill, pushing it so he can access what he wants—my tight, turned-on breasts. He traces hot kisses down the side of my neck and teases my nipples with his fingertips before fastening his mouth on one and feasting. I almost howl. I can feel the pressure of him at the apex of my thighs and all I can do is rock some more and moan. His hands work fast between us now. I hear the sound of the wrapper tearing, the hiss of breath as he rolls the protection down his erection. Am I really going to do this? *Hell yes.*

Nothing's ever felt like this. I don't think I'll feel anything like this again. My hunger just sharpens.

He pauses. 'Are you sure?'

I've never been more sure of anything. The wind whips outside and every so often lightning cracks but I don't care. I'm no longer scared. Impatient, I push forward, pressing onto him. But something isn't quite right and the sudden pain is intense. I freeze.

'Sweetheart?'

I chose not to tell him. I figured it doesn't matter. It's my business. But now I *can't* speak. I'm overwhelmed and all I want is for him to help me.

'You're so tight,' he mutters between clenched teeth. 'Has it been a while, darling?'

'Y-yes.' A half-truth isn't a lie, right?

I don't want him to stop. But right now I'm frozen because I don't know what I'm doing. I don't know how to get through this. It's a searing, tearing sensation.

'Let me help,' he grits.

'Yes, please.' I need it—him.

He pulls out. I whimper because that's not what I wanted at all. But he kisses me and he's so tender with my mouth. His fingers are tender too. Slow and teasing and he sweeps me back into that heat. I melt again and soften. He strokes, not just one finger inside me, but two, then three—pumping me, priming me with slow deliberation. It's so much and so good I almost come again. That's when he slides his fingers from me. I hiss in frustration.

'You're ready for me now,' he says, voice low.

'Yes…' I roll my hips.

He grips them hard and holds me still. I feel his broad blunt tip and heat surges within me. I slide as he thrusts so we collide and merge. I moan helplessly but this time the strangeness of the sensation is surpassed by surging pleasure. Pain hits then disappears as his guttural groan makes me slicker and I take more of him still. The sliding friction is easier—and exquisite. I take him to the hilt, feeling suddenly powerful, and squirm closer still.

Neither of us are quiet now. The sighs are from me. The grunts from him as he leads me into a rhythm that's intense and undeniable. My mind, my body, close around him.

'Dain,' I moan into the hot crook of his neck as I curl around him.

'Now you're there, darling,' he murmurs approvingly, cradling me closer. 'You did it, you've got me.'

'Yes.' I want him. *So* much.

He's big and he's strong and the dragging sensation as he moves inside me is mind-blowingly delicious. What began as an amusement—as funny and tender and little more than a tease—has become something far more intense. There was another thread beneath that lightness—a ribbon of deeper desire that's now pulled free. We move together. He smothers me with kisses. It's as if he's wanted to do this for all eternity and now he has the chance, he's consuming me.

'Oh, gorgeous,' he breathes against my neck over and over and over as I sway like a blossom in his hold. 'You're just gorgeous.'

I melt in the heat of his approval. My eyes water again for a totally different reason. This is nothing like I've ever dreamed. It's better. Hell, maybe I'm already dead and I'm in heaven because this is the best feeling in the world.

'I can't last much...' His voice is ragged and he's struggling for coherence and it's all the sweeter, hotter, dirtier.

All I can do is moan in reply. My eyes close. I feel enveloped—inside and out—in hot velvet and silky steel. The storm outside is forgotten. The swing of the car only adds to the sensation of fierce freedom. Of achieving an impossibility. I'm secure in his embrace yet it's the wildest moment of my life. Finally it overwhelms me. I cry out as I come so hard I don't know anything any more. There's total body annihilation. I hear his words—filthy and fierce— as he thrusts hard into me, harder than ever, and grips me to him. The moment is more sweet than I could have ever imagined possible.

I don't know how long it is later when I realise I'm slumped over him, my head resting on his chest. We're still intimately connected. I never want to move.

'Imagine if the cable breaks now,' he mutters. 'What a way to go though, right?'

'Embarrassing if people found us locked together,' I mumble.

He nudges me gently. 'Worth it? Not worth it?'

'So worth it.' I lift my head and smile at him.

In the dim light cast from his phone I see him smile back and—

A screeching sound startles me. The cabin jolts severely and suddenly descends a few metres along the cable. His grip on me tightens to stop me from falling from his lap. The cabin lights blink a couple of times and then return to full power and Dain's arms loosen. I scramble off him and quickly tug down my dress, refasten the buttons at the neckline and scramble for my panties. My cheeks burn. So do other parts of me.

There's no camera in the cabin—thank goodness—but there is an intercom and it suddenly crackles, emitting a calming pre-recorded message saying we'll be at the ground soon and not to panic.

Dain swiftly does up his trousers and retrieves his phone from the floor. His shirt is half unbuttoned, his face flushed. He looks more than dishevelled—dissolute. As he glances up at me his muscles visibly tighten. I almost liquefy into a puddle on the floor. Apparently I've discovered my inner nymph.

But I gulp air, striving for nonchalance. 'We should probably—'

His phone beeps with a series of messages. Then it actually rings.

He glances at the screen and answers immediately. 'Simone? You okay?'

I can hear his godmother's tone but can't make out what she's saying. My heart kicks. Family loyalty matters to me. Well, *some* of my family. I would never not answer an invitation or call if my sister Ava needed me.

'Fine. I'm fine.' His gaze is trained on me as he talks to her. 'Everyone up there okay?' He nods reassuringly at me as he listens to what she says.

I smooth my hair and sit back down, grab my backpack and hold it on my lap in front of me like a protective shield.

Dain ends the call with Simone. 'Talia—'

'No regrets,' I quickly whisper.

His phone rings again. I see his frustration at the interruption but I'm relieved and gesture for him to answer it. I don't want to talk about what just happened. I don't want to analyse it or ruin it in any way. He lives in a different country. He's a billionaire and I'm a barista. This is over.

We're at the bottom of the gondola before that second call ends, before I can believe it. I can't believe anything about tonight. As the doors slide open there are five huge guys in firefighting gear waiting for us. I take advantage of the crowd and chaos to escape.

'Talia!'

I ignore his call. I run into the night—taking control—because I don't want an awkward, embarrassing goodbye. There's nothing to say. This was a moment I'll never regret, a moment I'll always treasure.

But nothing will ever come of it.

CHAPTER FOUR

Dain

AS MY PILOT brings the jet in to land I gaze at the mountain to the right. I'm not in the cockpit—my licence is more hobby than necessity—but if I had to take over the controls, I could. The mountains are snowy and majestic, the southern lakes sapphire, yet it's the gondola complex glinting in the sunlight snagging all my attention.

It's almost a year to the day since I was trapped in a suspension car with an annoyingly unforgettable woman. Almost a year since I last had sex.

Yeah, I can't believe that either. Trust me, I'm not happy about it.

My sexual appetite has simply…dried up. When I returned to Australia, I met other women but never took any home. Opportunities they offered, I ignored. I worked harder and longer hours until basically becoming a workaholic hermit.

In the decade before this last year I had many lovers and remained on good enough terms with most. I was upfront with what I offered—never more than a few nights' ultra-discreet fling—private islands, private hotels, no prying eyes. Definitely no cameras.

But Talia ran straight into that stormy night—leaving me. I had to stop and thank that rescue crew. It couldn't have been more clear that she wanted to get away. I let her. I don't chase women down.

I did, however, invest in Simone's project. And eventually I did go back to that restaurant—two months after that searing night I braved that bloody gondola again. By then the entire hospitality staff had turned over. The chef—Kiri—had been headhunted and moved north. No one on shift the day I returned knew anything about who'd been on front of house that wild night. I figured that was fate telling me to quit. I wasn't about to walk around town going to every restaurant and café on a quest to track down a barista called Talia.

Okay, I did do that. Briefly. It didn't work.

Now I'm back in Queenstown. We broke ground on Simone's apartment building two months ago and I'm here to check progress. And okay, yes, I can't resist the possibility I might see her.

I now know her name is Talia Parrish. Yeah, as much as I loathe online platforms I fully social-media-stalked my way to that information three months ago in a moment of fury over my tragic existence of the last year. I found her channel. I'm not one for sharing anything online but frankly I found it a disappointment. All her recent videos are just hands and coffee art—very clever art, to be fair, but we don't get to see her face.

I can't forget her face. I've tried but she haunts me at night. Every night. Worse, memories of that encounter hit at the most inappropriate times. I've never been as unable to control my own thinking. Hell, right now my body hardens the way it does at the thought of her. Only her. Frustrating isn't the word.

I need to see her again. I need to put that haunting nymph to bed for good.

Maybe it's just that feeling of unfinished business. The way she slipped into that storm to get away from me grates. We'd gone through something in that cable car—something more than just a physical tryst—so her instant vanishing act felt like a betrayal of the connection—the trust. Yeah, I'm a fool. The people *closest* to me kept the most terrible secrets from me, why am I so bothered by some random woman running off?

Twenty minutes after our mid-morning landing I'm walking along the main street of Queenstown. It's post-card perfect and there are crowds of ski and snowboarding lovers everywhere. I want to wipe them all out of my way.

'We'll be back soon!'

I freeze. I recognise a husky edge in that call. I turn even though my heart has yet to pump another beat. A bell jingles as the door of a warm-looking café closes. A woman is walking away from it—away from me.

I stare after her. She's wearing a woollen hat but there's a brunette plait hanging partway down her back. She's wearing an enormous black puffer jacket. From here I can see one seam patched with a piece of black duct tape. Even so a feather escapes. Because it's bulky I can't tell her shape but she's about the right height. What little I can see of her legs is encased in dark blue denim. Her boots are leather but, like the jacket, patched and old.

There's no way it'll be Talia, but I follow anyway. I'm compelled. She walks with a gentle sway that's almost hypnotic. Swallowing, I mock my foolishness. Her head is down and I haven't seen her face but I can't shake the conviction that it's her so I follow her journey all the way to the public gardens at the edge of the lake. She doesn't walk with both arms at her sides. She's holding one in front of her. Has she hurt it in some way?

In the gardens she pauses and I stop, hanging back by a tree so she can't see me. There's almost no one around now but the view of the lake and back to the small town is beautiful. It's not warm enough to be outside for long but she bends—somewhat awkwardly—to brush a dusting of snow from the park bench. Her bulky jacket still shields her body from me but as she sits on the space she cleared I glimpse the side of her face. It's her. It really is her.

My jaw drops but I say nothing. It's eerily quiet aside from a bird or something chirping. But it's not a bird. It takes me a beat to realise it's the cry of a small child. A baby. Talia fusses with a woollen scarf or something and tucks her head down. After a few moments the crying stops and it slowly dawns on me. She's not just cradling that baby. She's breastfeeding it.

Shock paralyses me. I stand there beneath the tree, staring like some deranged stalker while her earlier words to whoever was in that café come back to me.

'We'll be back soon.'

We.

I'm good at maths. Always have been. But right now my brain is only focused on the fact that sometimes— just sometimes—one plus one can equal three. I don't know how old that baby is. I don't know what a roughly three-month-old baby would look like. But I'm guessing it wouldn't be big.

So she got pregnant—*when*? Oh, I know. I know *exactly*. My gut burns with intuition. It was late one stormy night when she was suspended metres high above a mountain. When she was in my arms. When we sought mindless bliss together.

It was almost a year ago. Which means it's almost a year that she's kept this from me. She's not just deceived me, she's *deprived* me. I'm devastated.

In the next second rage hits.

I already know how it feels to be shut out. When family deny you everything. That's why I'll never have one of my own. You can't trust anyone. But it's happened to me *again*.

I almost can't stand. I press my palm to the rough trunk of the tree I'm under. It's cold and gnarled and it digs against my skin. I breathe in the freezing air—slow and deep—until I'm cold again too.

She adjusts the way she's holding the baby. I don't hear her words exactly, but I do hear the loving tone. Something other than rage swamps me.

My controlled breathing was pointless. Now I'm burning inside—kicked alive—by instinct. Need. *Action.*

I walk towards her, letting my boots scrunch on the stones and the frosty fallen leaves. But she doesn't even lift her head. From the angle I approach them at I glimpse the baby. It's asleep. I see it's dark lashes flush against soft-looking chubby cheeks. Talia's eyes are closed too. She's pale but as beautiful as ever as she rests in the weakened sunlight. I stop only a few feet away but still she doesn't stir.

I'm so focused on her I've forgotten to blink. Shocked and disbelieving. My teeth ache from the cold. From the fierceness with which I've been clenching them.

'Talia?' My voice is raspy but I try again. 'Talia?'

Her eyes flash open. Her chin jerks up as undeniable and absolute horror flashes on her face. *'No!'*

CHAPTER FIVE

Talia

No.

My involuntary emotional outburst hangs in the air and I can't bite it back no matter how much I want to. I've long given up thinking he might appear at any moment and for a split second I hope I'm dreaming. But I'm not. He's here. And he's looking…

Furious. *Fine.*

Dain Anzelotti towers over me and, despite my terror, all I can do is soak in the sight. A year ago I thought he was handsome. I was wrong. He's jaw-dropping. He's not in a suit today but instead wearing that casual billionaire winter uniform—leather boots, well-cut jeans, form-hugging merino sweater, tailored jacket. The layers don't hide his lithe, muscular frame. The denim grazes his quads. The jacket emphasises his broad shoulders. But his blue gaze nails me to the bench.

I'm stunned into silence, into stillness. Yet as the seconds tick a tendril deep inside me stirs to life. I thought it dead, not dormant. The shocking lust that once led me to lose control completely. He says nothing but I feel utterly disadvantaged as he stares at me from above. I don't breathe as he, oh, so deliberately lowers his gaze to intently study his tiny son tucked against me. I fight the overwhelming urge to run. I know it would be futile.

I don't know Dain well. We were together for only a couple of hours. But I can tell he's leashed. But the emotion burgeoning within *me* is what's really scary. I lost all control with this man and it upended my life completely. I can't allow that to happen again.

'Who's this?' His voice is raspy.

I don't answer. I can't. Is he *playing* with me?

'Don't try to tell me he isn't yours,' he adds harshly. 'I can't imagine you'd breastfeed a friend's baby in the park.'

'You were *watching*?' I gape. 'How long have you been following me?'

'Twenty-four minutes. Since you walked out of that café.'

I'm stunned again. He followed me here. He stood and watched me feed Lukas. I feel exposed—it's such a personal thing. Ordinarily it would be natural for the father of my baby to watch me nurture our baby but Dain rescinded his right to that intimacy months ago. It's too late now. It *has* to be. I lift my chin and emotion betters my brain. 'What do you *want*?'

His blue eyes flash fire. 'What's the baby's name?'

Oh, please. 'I already told you in the messages I sent you months ago,' I spit my fury at him. 'Again in the photo taken when he was born.'

Dain stands very still. 'What messages?'

I glare up at him, refusing to believe that flare in his eyes. 'The emails.'

'Never got any.'

'Don't believe you.' But I'm quaking inside because I know, I *know* I didn't try hard enough. 'I sent them to every permutation of your email I could think of. I even sent them to the help desk listed on your company website.'

There were four actual messages sent to multiple addresses. All increasing in urgency. But I *stopped* sending them. I tried but then I quit after Lukas's birth. I gave Dain the shortest of chances. Because he never bothered to reply. I knew he wouldn't. He told me he wasn't a commitment kind of guy and I saw for myself that he wasn't and I decided I didn't need to chase harder. He wasn't interested. I don't want that for my child. I want to protect him. And myself. Because I know rejection. I know just how much it *hurts*.

Suddenly Dain's on his haunches in front of me and his tone is colder than the frosty air swirling around us. 'What's the baby's name?'

I stare into his blue eyes and am helpless to do anything but answer. 'Lukas.'

His indrawn breath is sharp. 'Spelt how?'

Yeah. Smart question. But I guess it proves that I did go on his company website. I did try to make contact a few times at least. Because Lukas was his grandfather's name. My throat tightens. 'You already know—'

'Humour me,' he says, too silkily. 'I think it's the least you can do.'

'Lukas. With a K not a C.'

Another sharp breath. 'And does little Lukas have a middle name?'

Hearing him say Lukas's name does something to me. I'm suddenly shaking inside—such a sentimental fool. I wanted my son to have a connection to his father even when his father didn't even want to know him. 'His full name is Lukas Dain Parrish.'

Dain's gaze slices through me. 'Parrish?'

'That's my name.'

'But he's my child.'

I brace and look right into his angry eyes. '*Our* child.'

I've already given him two of Dain's family names. It was for balance and frankly more than generous enough.

The image slides into my head again. The one I hate. I know Dain went straight from that liaison with me into the arms of another woman that night. Whether she was his girlfriend or not I don't know. I don't want to. The thought of being the 'other woman' sucks. The pictures I saw online that next morning made me feel sick. In fact I felt sick every time I so much as thought of him for weeks after. And I kept thinking of him. Kept feeling sick. Morning sickness, in fact. Because I'm an idiot.

'You didn't tell me.' His rage is less suppressed now.

'You ignored my messages. Why are you here?' I ask him again before he can deny getting them again. 'Why unannounced?'

Is it to startle me? Because if so, it's certainly worked.

He stands, towering again, embodying the huge, threatening shadow he's become in my life. 'You need to come with me,' he demands.

'I don't think so.'

'We need to talk.'

I'm suddenly furious. Does he think he can ignore my messages and then just turn up? I can't let him storm in and blow up my life when I've come through the worst days after giving birth. When I almost have a sustainable routine going.

'You've had plenty of time to talk to me. You've chosen not to.' I go stone cold inside. 'I messaged multiple times and you ignored them.'

But the blank denial in his eyes is so real, I falter. He's

shockingly pale. His breathing is uneven. To my eternal horror I *know* this is all news to him. But I push on because now I'm terrified. 'Your chance to be involved has been and gone.'

His cool gaze slides over my face and drops to the baby again. 'Wrong. This is the first I've...'

I don't want to believe him. But I do. And now I feel atrocious.

'Then why are you in Queenstown if not to see us?' I whisper.

'Checking on a project.'

It's business.

I'm incredibly—stupidly—hurt. It's purely because of fate that he's found us. I shouldn't have gone for a walk today. I should have gone upstairs to feed Lukas. Then he wouldn't have seen us. Disappointment slices into me. It's the destruction of the last flicker of hope I hadn't realised I still had. But I'm still weak enough to be attracted to him even when he's ignored me till now. That I could be this crushed—again—is appalling. I'm as vulnerable as my mother and being that gullible—falling for a wealthy, good-looking cheater—was something I'd promised myself I wouldn't do.

I tear my gaze from Dain and look down at my baby. He's tiny, precious, so vulnerable and I'm overwhelmed by the need to protect him. I don't want him hurt. Not the way I was. I'll do anything to shield him from the wounds of being unwanted. I lean closer to him and breathe in his sweet baby scent. He has his father's eyes. The midwife told me that baby's eyes are often blue at first but that they can change, but that hasn't happened yet, and I don't think it will. He has Dain's dark brown hair too. And his ability to consume every inch of my attention.

'We don't need your help,' I mutter.

'No? Then why are you sleeping on a park bench in the mid-morning, like you're a homeless person?'

'We were just getting some fresh air.' But I'm overly defensive because if it weren't for my boss, Romy, we *would* be homeless. I live above her café. I know it's not ideal. I work in the kitchen in the very early hours—baking the muffins and pastries for the day. I'm still building my channel and film at night in the café when it's closed. But Lukas is a demanding baby and I can't care for him at the café and disturb the customers downstairs during the day. That's why I take him for long walks along the waterfront.

Now that I'd fed him I was letting him sleep for a moment before tucking him properly back into his sling so I could walk back. But I'm tired. I've done today's baking. I've done my own work overnight so I snatch sleep in short shifts whenever I can. I'm doing okay and working my butt off to do better. Because I adore Lukas and I'll do whatever necessary to provide for him. But it's hard. Even so, I definitely don't want Dain's help now.

'Talia.'

Bleary-eyed, I glance up at him again. He's *beautiful*. It's like a boulder landing in my stomach—immobilising me. He's also determined. And fiercely strong—physically and mentally. Panic sweeps, darkening everything in the world except for him—as if he's in the damned spotlight—he's all I can see. And what I feel is overwhelming.

I liked him. A lot. But he—like everyone—let me down. I know that the only person I can ever really rely on is myself. Lukas is relying on me too.

And I know giving in to whatever Dain is about to demand will be dangerous. If he wins now, he'll think he can win always.

'Let's go to your home,' he says. 'We'll talk there.'

I don't want him to see how we're living. I don't want any of this. We live in different countries. We have vastly different lives. So I have no idea what he's going to want or how it's going to work. But I will stay in Lukas's life and so I have to be calm and stay in control. I have to do my best for my son.

I don't answer Dain verbally. I simply stand and start walking, cradling my precious son, hating the heat that's coursing through my body as this tall, devastating man wordlessly falls into step alongside me. Well, he stalks really—like a barely leashed predator. For the first time in months I feel revitalised—fury fills me with the energy I've been lacking in so long. As we walk I lift my head and breathe deep and when we finally arrive…

I'm ready to fight.

CHAPTER SIX

Dain

I'VE HAD ONE serious concussion in my life from a skiing accident when I was fourteen. Back then I lost three hours but right now I'm more stunned and confused than when I woke up and found myself in a hospital hundreds of kilometres from the ski field. Today it seems I've lost *months*. I can't see straight, let alone think. My thundering pulse deafens me to anything—any excuse—she might try to make.

She's had a baby. My *son*. And this is the first I've heard about it and that's only because I happened upon them by accident.

I barely register the walk back to the café. She leads me through the crowded tables to the rear. Behind a door marked *Private* there's a narrow flight of stairs. Climbing them, I feel the echo of that small storeroom where we first met. The room at the top of these stairs is even smaller. The first thing I see is a narrow bed. A baby bassinet is pulled up beside it. Everything is clean and neat but spare—it's minimal in decor, devoid of luxury. Bare necessities only.

Anger churns but desire adds a vicious twist right at the most wrong of moments. I want her on that bed. With me. Which is ridiculous because it's nowhere near big enough for the both of us. Yeah, cognitive function is fully impaired and anger is the safest option.

'How long have you lived here?' I growl.

'I need to change Lukas,' she mutters.

I watch. She's efficient as she cares for the baby. Of course she is. She's done this hundreds of times. I wouldn't know where to begin. My anger sharpens as she picks him up again. The betrayal is intense and when she smiles at the baby I snap.

'You need to start packing,' I hiss and shove my hands into my jacket pockets.

'Packing?'

'You can't stay another night here.'

It's noisy. It's tiny. Which is probably why she has to go for walks during the café's busiest hours. It's appalling.

She stares at me with such mistrust it burns. What did I ever do to deserve it? But I rein my resentment in. I need her to agree with me.

'We can't talk properly here. Not with people trying to enjoy their coffee downstairs.' And not in front of the child. 'Did I ever give you reason not to trust me, Talia? Because right now I feel like I'm the one who can't trust you, given you never told me I have a son.'

'I *tried*—'

'Exactly where did you supposedly send all those messages?' I ask.

'Don't you believe I sent them?' she whispers furiously. 'Why don't you check?'

'Why do you think I'm asking?' I snap back. 'A forensic IT search is about to be launched.'

She looks down at the baby and I see her striving to steady her breath. 'There isn't a direct email for you listed on your company website. You have no phone number.

Your social media profiles are non-existent. You're *very* well protected from the public.'

She's right. I push for as much privacy as possible. 'So you sent them to…?'

Coming from one of Australia's most wealthy families—plus being single—provides challenges. All emails are filtered but surely hers should have been flagged.

'I sent them to the information address.'

What did she say? How blunt was she? How many did she send? I can't shake the feeling that it wasn't as many as possible. 'You should have tried harder.'

She lifts her chin defiantly. 'Perhaps I should have gone to the *media*? Sold my story? Shamed you by saying we had sex in the middle of a thunderstorm and that as a result…' Her eyebrows lift.

I'm on fire inside at the thought of that—I'm too aware of the ravenous public appetite for personal drama. I would have *loathed* it but the truth would've got to me at last. 'Perhaps you should have,' I say more calmly than I'm feeling. 'It would have got my attention.'

'And destroyed *my* reputation—my career—in the process. I'd have become known as Dain Anzelotti's baby-mama. As far as I could tell, you weren't interested. I needed to protect my own earning potential.'

'You're a waitress.'

She glares at me but I'm unapologetic. 'No doubt you'll think it arrogant if I suggest that your being linked with me would only *enhance* your earning potential,' I add.

'You don't know anything about me.'

Not entirely true. I know some things. Quite a lot. I know the sound she makes when she's so hot she can't stand it any more. I know her scent. I know how tightly her hand can squeeze mine. I know her taste. But I don't trust her. I don't trust anyone.

'Right, and you know little about me—'

'I know plenty. I looked up who you were.'

I see condemnation in her eyes and my skin prickles. Has she seen the past—some of those stories about my parents? Is this why she's kept Lukas secret, because she's afraid I'll be as awful as my own parents were? 'And whatever you discovered put you off trying harder to contact me?'

'You don't want to settle down. You're used to getting what you want. Who you want. When you want.'

'And these are such insufferable qualities you think I shouldn't have any part in my son's life?'

She whitens.

But I'm angry with her judgement. Only at the same time she's right. I'm used to people doing what I ask them to. I'm used to being in charge of pretty much everything. Yet Talia Parrish only has to enter my mind and I lose control of my own damned body. I'm hard for her. I'm always hard for her. *Only* hard for her. And I hate it.

Stupid, *stupid* chemistry.

Once was not enough. That's all.

Memories flood my mind. That night was a set of circumstances where adrenalin was pumping and the satisfaction—a life-threatening moment made earthly pleasure extreme. I had to hurriedly get rid of that condom. There was no time to check it properly but I've often remembered her tension when I first entered her. Crazy as it is, I suspect she was a virgin. But surely not.

She lifts her chin. 'I don't want him confused by all the women in your life.'

I narrow my gaze. '*Neither* of us will parade lovers in front of him. I don't want him to have a revolving door of people he thought might care about him only to be disappointed.'

Her eyes widen. 'I agree.'

'Fancy that,' I say coolly. 'We might agree on more once we really get going.' I drag in a breath. 'I can adjust accordingly, Talia. I hope you're able to do the same.' Her assumptions about my character annoy the hell out of me. 'Why did you stop trying to reach me?'

She stands stiffly. 'It was clear you weren't interested.'

'I didn't *know*.' I bite the words.

She could have tried again. Tried harder. I'm furious with myself for ignoring that nagging feeling about her for so long.

'I want you to come to Australia with me.' I blurt, losing the ability for fine negotiations.

I need privacy and time to get my head around this and there's only one place I know where I'm sure I can get it. My place is a fortress.

'No.' Shock whitens her face. 'Not possible.'

I just stare at her.

'I don't have a passport. Nor does Lukas.' She squares her shoulders. 'That's why I couldn't travel to try to see you when I realised I was pregnant.'

She's determined to throw roadblocks up. She didn't have the money either. That's evident. Defensive as hell and I'm not coping with it as well as I should.

'We'll get them expedited.'

'That'll make them more expensive.'

'Hardly a problem for me.'

'Billionaire. Right,' she says scornfully. 'I'm not leaving New Zealand. My *life* is here.'

My gaze drops to the baby and I see her defensively tighten her hold on him. She looks scared.

'And *my* life is *there*.' I pause. 'Lukas belongs to us both.'

'So what are you suggesting? Should we chop him in two?'

I dislike myself intensely at this moment. She really didn't want me to know. She doesn't want my input with Lukas. That hurts. I'm independent. In control. I've had no control here in this. I grit my teeth at the realisation that I'm not going anywhere without her. 'I'll delay my return to Australia. We need time to sort this out. But I'd like you to stay with me so we can take advantage of Lukas's nap times to talk.' I look down at her. 'I'm trying to compromise, Talia.'

She hesitates. 'It'll take me a while to pack. Give me the hotel address and I'll meet you there.'

'I'll sit down and hold him while you get on with it.'

She doesn't expect that. Honestly, I've surprised myself too. I'm not exactly an experienced baby-handler and I give a mutter of thanks that one of the women in HR returned recently to show off her new baby and they made a deal of me cradling her baby. It means I've the smallest notion of what to do now.

Honorary fun uncle was the extent of what I was aiming for in life. I have no siblings, so real uncle was never going to happen. Nor was having a wife. That last one still isn't.

Talia doesn't move and I stare at her. Frustration surges at her obvious reluctance. I take a seat on the edge of that too small bed and hold my arms out. She finally steps forward. Our hands brush as she places Lukas into my arms. I look down at him and it's a good thing I already took a seat because my legs suddenly empty of strength.

He's a beautiful boy. Curling eyelashes. Unblemished pink cheeks. He's tiny and so light that I'm terrified I'll crush him—my *son*.

My heart stalls. I never wanted this—never so much as imagined it. But now he's here and in a split second of clarity I know I'll never, ever give him up. He's mine. I'm awash with a feeling unlike any other. Protectiveness obliterates all other emotion. I'll do anything to ensure his safety. He'll be with me. Always. Involuntarily I glance up at her and our gazes mesh.

So will she.

A whisper of equal clarity that I want to reject. Other feelings surge. I focus on the anger. I can't trust her but I need her—*Lukas* needs her. And I'm going to need defences to deal with her.

Her deep brown eyes are like pools—sombre and intense.

'Something wrong?' My voice has roughened to sandpaper.

'No.' Abrupt, she glances away.

It's a lie.

'Talia—' I raise my voice but break off as I remember. I look down at the innocent baby in my arms and then look back up at her. 'I'm not fighting with you in front of Lukas. Not ever.'

CHAPTER SEVEN

Talia

THERE'S SUCH SAVAGERY in his whisper I step back but I can't help looking at them again. He's still studying Lukas, intently absorbing every detail as if he's never seen a baby before. I'm unable to move—literally arrested by the sight of my son and his father finally together. Lukas looks tiny as Dain carefully cradles him. There's such a 'them' about this moment—an intimacy I'm intruding on. This should have happened three months ago. It should have happened the day Lukas was born.

Loss hits me, yearning and, yes, remorse. Each blow knocks the breath from my body. The regret isn't only for the delay in this, but the realisation that *we're* not a family. My son doesn't have that. I don't have that—a partner to offer not just support and security but love.

I remember the day of Lukas's birth. I missed Dain—I wanted to hold his hand through the delivery. I haven't let myself think about that since. But I cried, alone—and scared.

He's angry with me. He's right to be. I ran away from the conflict—the rejection—just as my mother always did. I already know I wouldn't fit into his world. Wealthy people like him live on a planet that has no place for me except as an employee. I've been told in no uncertain terms, repeatedly by one of the rich jerks my mother fell for and by his daughter, who I thought was my friend. But I was merely her charity case.

I turn away, angry with him too. For never replying. Never returning to Queenstown. For having other priorities in his life. But we were only ever supposed to have been a moment and it's unreasonable of me to have wanted otherwise.

I pack quickly. I'm used to taking only what I can carry so I'm pretty minimalist. It's the extra things for Lukas that slow me—his nappies and clothes, his few toys, his bassinet and bedding.

'You don't have a pram?'

I shove a toy into my backpack and answer shortly. 'I use a sling for now.'

I would've loved a pram or buggy to take him on walks but there's no way I could get a pram up the stairs and there's nowhere to store it in the café. Besides which, I couldn't afford it. It's less than five minutes before everything is stowed.

Dain carefully passes Lukas back to me. 'I need to make a couple of arrangements.'

It's a relief that he puts his intense focus onto his phone. He taps several messages before making a call.

'Do you have a car seat for him?' He interrupts his flow to ask me.

I nod, I was loaned one. I'm glad Romy isn't on shift at the café, so I don't have to explain anything to her in person. I'll leave a message for her in a bit.

Ten minutes later I carry Lukas and my backpack downstairs. Dain carries Lukas's bag and his bassinet. On the pavement, a driver waiting beside a gleaming black car hastens forward to assist. I don't know if I'll be coming back. Again, that's something that's all too familiar.

Bitterness wells and I blink back tears. I'm used to upheaval like this and I'm a survivor, but I didn't want Lukas to experience it ever. I want him to have stability and *security*. So I have to work this out with Dain.

I've never forgotten that night and part of me is still deeply attracted to him—the hormonal, basic breeding instinct part. You'd think it would have been satisfied already. Yep, I'm a fool. It's not that I don't think relationships can ever last but a guy like Dain—rich and entitled—isn't a commitment king. Yet I went with him anyway—blinded by looks and charisma and the impetuousness sparked by that stormy night. And if it had been for just that one wild night I might've got away with it, but for my precious child.

It's a twenty-minute, awkward-silence-filled drive out of town.

I frown. 'I thought we were going to a hotel?'

Instead we pull up at a stunning mansion on a large section. Established trees shield it from the road, yet once we're inside I clock the amazing views of the vast landscape.

'This place belongs to a friend,' he says.

'Does she hire it out?'

'What?' He looks blank. 'No.'

I could kick myself. She's wealthy—another world where you can have a holiday home bigger than most people's houses and keep it empty most of the year round. I've no reason or right to be jealous yet the feeling rising within me is nothing but ugly. I make myself say something polite. 'It's beautiful.'

'We'll have privacy here,' he says crisply.

He cares so very much about privacy. I wonder what

happened to make him value it so acutely. Is it simply the pressure of being a high-net-worth individual? That poor-rich-boy thing? That isn't happening to Lukas.

There was an image of Dain and his grandfather on the history section of the company website. Nothing of his parents. Dain looked about eleven in the photo.

'You don't need anything else for Lukas?' he asks as he carries in the bags. 'I thought there were all kinds of things babies needed, but this doesn't seem like much.'

Shame burns. I don't have the money for anything more than the basics.

'We'll get whatever else we need in Australia,' he says.

'Don't think that by repeatedly mentioning it, I'll suddenly agree to move.' I follow to see where he's taking Lukas's bed. 'I'm used to sleeping near him.'

'Sure.' He walks forward. 'While we're here, he's in the room between each of ours.'

Lukas is restless and needs some playtime. I lay him on the warm rug in front of the wood-burner that was lit before we arrived. I kneel beside him and pull out his favourite rabbit toy to play and let him kick out his legs.

Dain appears in the doorway but doesn't venture in. 'He'll be okay if we watch him from here while we talk?'

My stomach sinks. I feel as if I've been summoned to the principal's office. He's watching Lukas but as I approach his gaze lifts. Heat crawls over me. Suddenly clumsy, I almost trip over my own feet.

'What's the project you have in Queenstown?' I mumble to distract us both from my humiliating loss of co-ordination.

'The new apartments by the golf course. That's why I was here a year ago. Simone wanted my investment.'

I know the ones. According to the sign they're all sold already and they've barely begun building them.

'Why did you run off so quickly that night?' he asks bluntly.

'I had another job to get to.'

'Wasn't it cancelled because of the storm? Surely the bar was closed after the power cut? You could have taken two minutes to say goodbye.'

Because *goodbye* was all there should've been to say. I don't answer and he doesn't wait long.

'When did you find out you were pregnant?'

He's going direct. I've imagined this conversation so many times but I still struggle to explain. 'I'd been working long hours and just thought I was irregular. It wasn't till I started showing that I…' *Completely panicked.* 'That I did a test.'

'Were you taking care of yourself?'

I stiffen. 'I don't party, if that's what you're worried about.'

There's a rueful twist to his lips I don't quite understand.

'I'm more worried about the hours you work.'

I don't respond because ironically it's right this second that I realise how horribly tired I am. I've been filming late at night, baking early morning, caring for Lukas round the clock all while recovering from his birth.

'You knew the baby was mine?' His voice lowers.

My shrug is non-committal because I don't want to tell him that he's the only person I've ever slept with.

His gaze flickers. 'You didn't consider ending the pregnancy?'

Maybe he thinks I'm irresponsible given I'm in not in the best position to care for him? Once I was past that initial amazement I was elated. 'Even if I'd found out sooner, I wouldn't have done anything differently.'

'Including not trying harder to contact me?'

The truth is I'll do *anything* to keep my baby, but I can't tell him that because it will give him absolute power over me. Even though he'll likely have that anyway, given he has resources I can't compete with. I'll have to compromise.

'I love Lukas,' I say huskily, my heart aching. 'I tried to contact you. When you didn't reply I stopped.'

'Your family helped?'

I'm thrown. 'My what?'

'Did they support you through the pregnancy?' He frowns. 'Your parents?'

I'm so stunned I'm too honest in my answer. 'I haven't had parental support in years.'

'They're dead?'

'It's been so long since I saw my father he might as well be,' I mutter. 'My mother is around but…'

'You're not close.'

My mum's way of coping with anything bad is to uproot and ship out. Unfortunately bad stuff happens to her frequently and usually involves some jerk. She's been desperate for someone to depend on for my whole life and made way too many bad choices in that search. We had to move far too often, which impacted on my and Ava's friendships and our education—not that Mum cared about those things. Or us.

But I did. I'd already been working part-time for years to supplement what little money Mum made and I didn't want Ava to have to start over in yet another school. I dropped out and worked full time, that way I could afford a tutor to extend her. The school turned a blind eye to the fact no one turned up to parent-teacher interviews. But I don't explain all this to Dain, he's frowning enough as it is.

'I've been supporting myself since I was a teenager.' I lift my head proudly. 'I work several jobs and work hard.' It's never been easy but I've supported Ava for years and now Lukas too. 'My social media channel is building and income is trickling in from that. I don't want to lose momentum.'

'You don't need to make money,' he dismisses. 'You can delete the channel.'

'Pardon?' If I had hackles, they'd be on end. 'My career matters to me.'

'You never have to work again if you don't want to.'

'What? And be completely dependent upon you?' I'm appalled and a horrifying thought occurs to me. 'I don't want to be a kept woman. Certainly not your wife.'

Would he be that old-fashioned?

'Have I asked you to be?' he drawls.

Of course he hasn't. I'm not the society sort of wife Dain Anzelotti would have. The beautiful model with the famous family pedigree that he was photographed with minutes after being with me, however, she'd be perfect. I grit my teeth.

'I'm not interested in marriage,' he adds.

'That night you were unashamedly anti-kids too.'

'What's happened isn't Lukas's fault. I'll be there for him.'

'What does that even mean?' I ask smartly. 'Will you tolerate his existence? He won't be too much of an inconvenience?' I step forward. If there's no commitment between us there's an easy escape for Dain and I already know no one can be relied on. 'You get one chance,' I mutter fiercely. 'If you ever walk out on Lukas then you're out of his life for good.'

'Right back at you.' He steps forward to go toe to toe with me. 'I don't believe in marriage.' He sneers through the word. 'We'll have an unbreakable, legally enforceable *contract*. It doesn't need to be difficult or emotive. We'll agree to terms and we'll get on with it.'

He means an access plan. He means a dictate on where we live and how long for. What school Lukas will go to. Which doctor. Every aspect of his life will be agreed in advance between us. I'm going to lose full autonomy and have to agree with a man used to getting his own way. He's watching me closely and the longer I remain silent, the bigger the storms grow in his eyes.

'My parents' marriage was a mess,' he suddenly whispers. 'I was weaponised. Victimised. Blamed. That's never happening to Lukas. We'll work everything out between us well ahead of time so he never has to feel—'

He breaks off and takes a sharp breath. He glances away from me to look at our baby on the soft rug.

He doesn't want to tell me more. Fair enough. There's plenty I don't want to tell him either.

'Okay, we'll work it out,' I agree softly. With no marriage. No dependency. 'We both want the best for him.'

The problem is we might not always agree on what that 'best' will be.

CHAPTER EIGHT

Dain

I NEVER DISCUSS my family, but this morning has been shock after shock and my new reality is so far from normal I'm spinning. I glance at Lukas to ground myself and remember the priority here. He has my eyes and colouring. But knowing that Talia stopped trying to contact me grates nerves already stripped raw. Instinct screams at me to scoop him up and squirrel him to the safety of my own home. But instinct doesn't eliminate ignorance—I've no idea how to care for a baby, how to create the safety I fundamentally crave for him. It's all emotion and no experience. I don't like it. I don't like any of it. Especially the fact that I can't do this without her. And I'm angry with her. Yet every damn time I glance at her every damn atom within me heats. I *can't* lose control. She hasn't allowed me any in all this and that's not something I can tolerate. Family drama upended my life before and I'll never let it happen again.

She says she doesn't want anything from me, yet I see that same heat I feel in her eyes when she looks at me. She can't hide it and I'm tempted to use whatever power I might have to engineer an advantage. But then I remember how quickly she ran that night. Was it me or is it something within herself?

It must be me. And it must be bad. Because it's unbelievable that not even my money was a motivation for her to try harder.

Lukas begins to cry. While I freeze, Talia steps forward to pick him up.

'I need to top him up and hopefully he'll sleep again.' She looks around for a chair to nurse him in.

I can't stand to watch that sweet intimacy again so I walk away. I check the rooms, fiddle with the heating, attending to the basics—shelter, warmth…food? I grab my phone, start a list and make an order. Gradually I feel calmer. I call my legal team then my primary assistant. There's a huge amount to arrange and not a lot of time to do it.

As I finish the fourth call I see a car pulling into the driveway. Relieved, I head out to meet the delivery guy and carry the bags back to the kitchen.

Talia appears in the kitchen just as I'm serving up. The shadows beneath her eyes have deepened since I first saw her this morning, plus she has a pinched look as if she has a headache. While Lukas is thriving, she needs replenishing. I clench my jaw to crush back my growl of frustration. 'He's asleep?'

She nods and I glimpse how bony her shoulders are.

I jerk a thumb towards the kitchen counter. 'Sit. Eat.'

She glares but mercifully doesn't argue.

Lunch is a simple spread—warm soup, crunchy bread, soft butter. As she eats, I watch colour slowly return to her cheeks. I eat as well. But it feels more dangerous to be around her without Lukas.

'You should rest,' I mutter as soon as she's done. 'You look like you need it.'

She looks startled, then indignant.

'Go,' I say gruffly. 'Take a break.'

She meets my gaze. Yeah, it's definitely more dangerous to be near her without Lukas. But apparently she feels the same because she scuttles away.

In the late afternoon my team get in touch. They've expedited the information I requested and I print the file they've sent. The space for the father's name is blank but the baby's name gives it all away. *Lukas Dain Parrish.*

Just as she said. It would have been easy enough for her to discover my grandfather's name. It's in the brief family history I allowed on the company website to sparsely furnish the company's 'story'.

An hour later I put the printout on the kitchen table in front of her. 'You didn't name me on the birth certificate. I understand that if I were named, then I would be a guardian. As guardian I'll then have some say in my own child's upbringing.' I breathe out but my chest is tight. 'My lawyers filed a declaration of paternity.'

Her hands tremble, and my teeth clench because I hate her obvious fear of me.

'I want to establish Lukas's legal rights as well as my own. If anything happens to me, Lukas inherits.' I try to explain my reasons. 'No question. No delay. Plus he gets everything he should have had from the start.'

'We don't need things.'

'*You* don't have to have anything from me,' I say pointedly. 'Lukas, however, is different.'

'You sure you don't want a DNA test?'

My skin tightens. She thinks I have any doubt? 'Eventually. My lawyers will insist on it but you and I already know.'

Her eyes widen.

'What's weird to me is that you wanted him to have a family connection yet barely tried to contact me. It's hard to understand.' Was money really no motivation? Because that's not how it usually works in my world.

She bites on her lip. 'I don't like having to rely on any-one.'

Trust issues. Yeah, we have those in common. I offer the faintest smile. 'You're still a control freak, then?'

'Leopards. Spots.' She drops her gaze.

'Born that way or forged?' I ask.

She freezes.

'I was forged,' I mutter.

'Your parents?' She jerks a nod, answering before I do. 'Ditto.'

Right, we have dysfunctional families in common too. 'What is it you don't like about me, Talia?' I can't believe I've asked.

'You're used to being in charge.' She doesn't deny it.

I bristle. 'So are you.'

Her glance is pointed. 'Not on the same level.'

Lukas cries and she goes to him before I can blink.

I make more arrangements. Sort flight schedules. Offload my over-full diary for the next couple of weeks.

Dinner is desultory. She glances at me a few times but doesn't break the silence. I glance at Lukas and don't know where to begin with him.

She takes him to bathe and get ready for bed and I don't interfere. Given I'm going to need time away from the office, I draft a tonne of instructions. It's late when I turn out the light and the house is silent.

Three hours later I'm lying there still wide awake when I hear him crying.

I get up and pull on my jeans. The house is warm enough

not to bother with anything else. I step into the doorway and see her pacing around the small room with him. She looks exhausted. And beautiful.

'Is it like this every night?' I ask with clenched teeth.

'He's a little baby.' She defends him with quiet ferocity. 'He has no concept of time. And he's hungry. He's growing fast.'

There's a proud tilt to her head. I didn't mean to be critical, just curious. But we seem to read the worst into every interaction we have. I turn and stalk to the kitchen. Lukas can only keep growing like that as long as Talia is well rested and well-nourished herself. I grab a few crackers, slice cheese, slice an apple, make a milky hot chocolate and throw the lot onto a tray I find. It's hardly pretty but it's something.

I stomp—silently—back to the bedroom we're using as his nursery. Now Talia's curled up on the narrow bed and Lukas is in her arms. I clench my fists to ride out the urge to drop to my knees at her damned feet in awe and instead set the tray beside her so she can reach it easily.

'I don't need—'

'Don't,' I say sharply.

She glances at me—equally sharply—and says nothing more.

I lean back against the wall and glare at her. She sighs heavily, rolls her eyes and grudgingly picks up a cheese-topped cracker. My muscles don't ease any until she's onto her third. She sips the warm milky chocolate.

Eventually she puts him back into the small bassinet. He stirs and she rests her hand on him for a moment of reassurance. Then she straightens and silently steps out of the room. I follow her. Before I think I reach out and take her arm, turning her to face me. In the dim light of the hallway her eyes are huge. They draw me in—so rich and unfathomable.

Desire engulfs me. Paralyses me. She basically hid my son from me. Because of her I've missed out on so much. But her soft skin is beneath my fingertips and I can't resist stroking her lightly with my thumb. Just the once. I see her skin flush, hear her breathing race. Her response is instant—just like that night in the gondola.

I can't speak. I just stare at her and inwardly battle the overpowering desire to pull her close and kiss her and touch her everywhere.

'You don't have to get up every time he cries,' she mumbles.

Rejection. Denial. Again. It's as aggravating as hell that she won't let me help her.

'You do.' I flinch. 'You have. For months.'

As she stares up at me something changes in her expression. Her whole body seems to tremble. 'I'm sorry.'

The words I've been waiting for all day finally emerge from her but weirdly I don't want to hear them. Not *now*. Because they make me feel something—*want* something— that I know in my bones is dangerous. I'm suddenly, sharply vulnerable. I cannot trust her. I cannot take her in my arms. But I'm so tempted. Frustration is an inferno.

'Go to bed,' I growl.

I release her too roughly. I almost push her away. I have to because in the next heartbeat I'd have hauled her close and damned myself.

Her swift steps are silent on the soft carpet. Her door closes with the faintest click. The speed with which she leaves me is both relief and agony.

I slowly uncurl my fist—holding back from grabbing her again has my hand cramping. I have no idea how I'm going to get through this.

CHAPTER NINE

Talia

I SLEPT BADLY and it wasn't because Lukas had woken more than once. Dain had been thoughtful—grumpy, but thoughtful—in the middle of the night. I wasn't able to get back to sleep at all because the reality of my position is very clear. It's taken less than twenty-four hours back in his presence and I'm willing to do almost anything he wants. I don't deserve his attention but I want it. And last night—for a moment—I had it. But he stepped back right at the moment I would've surrendered. He doesn't want me any more. Or maybe he doesn't *want* to want me. And he doesn't trust me.

But I'm going to go with Dain to Australia. I'm going to agree to almost anything he wants to ensure Lukas has the best from us both. Because Lukas comes first. But it's not only Lukas depending on me, I have Ava too and I have to do my best for her as well. If I leave she'll be alone. Which means taking a risk. Enraging Dain seems less terrifying now I've seen him with Lukas.

He's *interested* in his son and he wants the best for him. Yep, he might've had some tough times in his own child-hood that he doesn't want to open up about, but he wants to protect Lukas from anything similar. Fine by me. It's awful to admit, but I'm actually a little jealous of the way he looks at Lukas, how carefully he held him. I need to get over that. And knowing I don't have his trust, I figure I might as well do the worst and hopefully ensure Ava is okay as well.

I find him sitting at the kitchen table. There's a coffee beside him and the remnants of an omelette on a plate. My heart thunders and I feel cold, but I do the thing I promised myself I never would.

'You said you're a billionaire.' My voice cracks. I clear my throat and make myself continue. 'Is it all tied up in assets or do you have access to cash?'

Surprise lights his eyes. 'I can access cash. Why?' He cocks his head and surveys me steadily. 'How much do you need?'

I don't hesitate. 'Quarter of a million.'

'Uh…' He does hesitate. Briefly. 'No more, no less?'

'Quarter of a million. Cash. Upfront.'

'Or…?'

I swallow. 'Or I'm not going with you. Nor is Lukas.'

It's a bluff but one I have to make.

To my astonishment he doesn't instantly get angry. He blinks but the smallest quirk tilts his lips. Surely he's not *amused*?

'How will you stop me from taking him?' he asks blandly. 'And you, for that matter. You know I could bundle you both onto my jet and—'

'You're not a bully. You're not a criminal. And you don't have passports for either of us yet,' I say.

'The passports are less than twenty-four hours away and if you think I'm such a straight-up good guy why didn't you try harder to let me know you'd had my son?'

I don't want to admit my shame. I take a breath. 'This is my price. I won't ask for anything more. Not for me. Ever. But I need all of it. Upfront. Before leaving.'

'You want it in unmarked dollar bills? Untraceable bags?' His smile deepens.

I purse my lips. I need to remain serious so he finally gets that this isn't a joke. 'Bank transfer will be fine.'

'Sure.' He keeps his gaze drilled on me as he pulls his phone from his pocket. 'I need your account details.'

He says it so matter-of-factly I just stare for a moment.

'You're doing it *now*?'

'You want the money, don't you?'

I fumble for my phone and pull up my banking app and read the numbers to him.

He taps his screen for a few moments then glances up at me. 'The money's gone through.'

I just gape at him. 'What?'

'Refresh your app,' he says. 'It should be there.'

I really don't want to believe him, but I do it. And there it is. I break into a sweat. My account has never seen so many zeros. There's a quarter of a million dollars—plus the meagre few hundred I had saved in there. I drag in a breath but still feel as if I'm suffocating. The sweat trickles down my spine as I tap the screen to forward the payment to Ava right away. I'll call her and explain it all later. I just want that money out of my account now. Because I feel bad about this. So bad. I'm barely aware that Dain's now standing beside me, silently observing over my shoulder.

But the payment doesn't go through. I frown at the 'transaction denied' message.

'I put money into that account all the time,' I mutter. 'Why won't they let me do it today?' I tap the app and try again. A big bright red alert message appears at the top.

'It's been "blocked for unusual activity".' I read it aloud in frustration. 'I have to phone them. Or go into a branch and take photo ID with me.'

'Your bank is right to query such a large transfer,' Dain says, way too calmly for me to handle.

'Because I'm usually so destitute an amount like this has to be some kind of fraud?' My eyes fill. I was so close and I'm frustrated. And I'm kind of blown away that he's just done that with no questions asked and I'm horrified with myself for asking him to in the first place. I feel as though I'm about to vomit.

Dain pushes me into the seat and hunches down before me.

'Breathe,' he instructs calmly. 'Just breathe.' Reaching up, he wipes a rogue tear from my cheek.

'How about you just tell me what it's for?' he says after a few moments. 'Are you in trouble—is it debt collectors?' He growls. 'I can help, Talia. I have a whole team of people who can help. It's not hard for me. I have an appalling amount of privilege. Let me help you with whatever the problem is.'

I stare at him and simply feel worse.

'Because there's obviously a problem,' he adds. 'Talia?' he prompts.

'It's for my sister,' I blurt.

His eyes widen. 'Sister?'

'Yes.'

'I didn't know you had a sister.'

I shoot him a look. 'Swapping life stories isn't a favourite pastime for either of us.'

'Right.' He almost smiles again. 'So she's in debt?'

'No. That's the point. I don't want her to be.' I breathe in slowly, frustrated because I'm explaining this backwards.

'She's a student. This is for her fees, her flat, her food for the next few years. She's in her second year of med school and she wants to specialise and—'

'That's a long expensive road ahead.'

'Exactly. She can't work while studying. She needs to concentrate fully. I don't want her to worry—'

'You've been supporting her for years,' he interrupts. 'Because neither of your parents help.' He suddenly rises and grabs his phone from the table. 'Give me her bank details.'

'What?'

He flips my phone around and copies the account number for Ava. I just stare at him, too sluggish and sickened to believe what I'm seeing.

A few minutes later he flips the phone back towards me. 'There's quarter of a million in her account now.'

As *well* as the quarter million in mine.

'Your bank lets you do that no problem?' I stammer. *'Twice?'*

The man had access to half a million dollars just like that?

I feel even more nauseous. 'Now I have to transfer all that back to you. But I have to go to the bank to—'

'Leave it,' he says shortly. 'Doesn't matter.'

'You're not *buying* me, Dain.' Even though I've basically just asked him to.

'Never dreamed that would be possible.' He suddenly chuckles. 'You're the one who demanded payment before leaving.'

'I'm not keeping that money in my account. Only the money for Ava and I'll pay that back. Eventually.'

He sighs and rolls his eyes. 'Whatever will help you sleep.'

But I feel worse.

'You might want to phone her before she calls her bank thinking there's been some sort of mistake and asks them to reverse it.' He draws a breath. 'You'll want to see her before we leave the country. We can—'

'No!' I shake my head furiously and the truth spills out before I think to stop it. 'She doesn't know about Lukas.'

'You haven't told your sister you've had a *baby*?' He frowns. 'I thought you were close.'

'We are.' But I have to explain more. I want him to understand his money isn't going to be wasted. 'I didn't want her dropping out to help me.'

'Yet that's what you did for her.'

'I never dropped *in*. I always worked. I never…' I shake my head, frustrated that I'm not explaining this well enough to wipe that frown off his face. 'Ava's amazing. Like really, really amazing. I didn't want her jeopardising her future and that's what she'd do if she knew—'

'How much you're struggling.'

I glare at him. 'I've worked too hard for too long to get her into the position she's in now.'

He glares right back at me. 'Your sister should know you've had a baby. Just as your baby's father should.'

It hits. Hard.

'You really do like keeping everything within your very tight control,' he says.

I don't know why he's so bothered by this. 'I was doing it for *her*.'

His mouth thins. 'No, you were controlling. Not involving her in any decision to help you or not. She'll be angry with you for keeping this from her.'

'That's a price I'm willing to pay because *her* future is too important. I was going to tell her once I had things more secure.'

'Fortunately things are more secure now. We'll visit her before we leave.'

I stare at him.

It didn't occur to me that visiting her would even be an option. I'm used to packing up and clearing out without any chance to say goodbye. The moment my mother decided, that was it—all hands on deck to put our few things into bags before they were forgotten. We always left as if a killer were at our heels.

Dain misinterprets my hesitation. 'Surely you don't want to leave the country without seeing her?'

My heart's in my throat. I would *love* to see her. I've missed her so much in these months that I've kept away from her. 'Are you sure?' I ask hesitantly. 'You don't mind?'

His jaw drops. 'I'm not a monster, Talia,' he mutters bleakly. 'I'm not going to force you to pack up and leave the country without saying goodbye to your family or friends first.'

I hear the hurt in his voice. 'I… I just…'

'Think the worst of me.'

'Of most people,' I correct. My heart squeezes. It isn't only him.

'Well.' He watches me. 'You can ask me for anything.'

To my total mortification my face heats and I can't even mumble a response. The things I really want to ask from him are way too…way too…*wild*.

CHAPTER TEN

Dain

'YOU WERE ABLE to lean on me that night in the gondola,' I point out to her, trying to soften my tone. How can I be fascinated and furious with her at the same time?

'That was a life-threatening situation,' she mutters.

The tips of her ears are scarlet again.

What's it going to take to get her to trust me again in any small way? Because I'm trying here. She's just demanded an outrageous sum of money and I've not batted an eyelid and supplied it immediately—although admittedly my motivation was mostly to confound her. But I desperately want her to open up more. I know she's ballsy and bristly but when she laughs—which is too rarely for my liking—she's a delight.

It's shocking enough that she hadn't properly tried to contact me about Lukas, but that she hasn't told her own sister about him either is blowing my mind—even when she insists they're close. And it touches a wound of my own. Not being told my grandfather was terminally ill—on the pretext of protecting me—is something I've never forgiven my family for.

'My assistant found the messages you sent and forwarded them to me,' I say.

She watches me warily.

'Overzealous spam folders and weak double checks in play there. There weren't as many as I'd thought. You didn't discuss the pregnancy in the first couple.'

'Of course I didn't, that was personal.'

Part of me appreciates her discretion. But her first two loosely worded messages—I need to get hold of Dain. We met one night—didn't pass the spam/stalker test. The last was too generic—I've had a baby—even with the photo attached.

'You could have tried harder,' I say. 'You should have.'

She could have tried to contact Simone. There were several avenues she chose not to go down.

'What were you so afraid of?' I ask.

Her skin pales. 'You have a lot more to offer him than I do.'

'You're his mother.'

'That doesn't always mean much.'

An element in her voice makes me wince. 'Do you struggle to accept help from anyone?'

'I took help from Romy.'

Minimal help that she paid back by working for her—making cakes and coffee. 'But you won't take it from me.'

'There are other complications between us.'

My gut twists. I'm tempted to sort those other complications out. I can't help wondering if there was any other man in her life after me. I shouldn't be thinking on it. I'm hardly about to tell her I've been celibate since sleeping with her. Besides, I have the feeling she won't believe me.

Too late I realise my glib display of outrageous wealth has backfired. If I make a move on her now she might not feel able to say no. She might think I've *bought* her. That's just *ick*. I was so determined to be flippant. To prove nothing's a problem. No demand too outrageous. I didn't think through the implications.

I can't allow her to kiss me as some kind of repayment. But all I want right now are her kisses. And isn't this just the way it is with Talia? Contrary. Confounding. My muscles bunch and twitch. I just want to tear her clothes away. Mine too.

It's a relief to hear Lukas's cry coming from the nursery.

I go to him immediately. I croon ridiculously as I pick him up and try to soothe him. I turn about the room and see she's followed and is watching me. The look in her eyes isn't worry. It's heat. She can't stop looking. Despite my edginess I keep talking nonsense to Lukas to keep him settled because to my amazement it seems to be working. There's a feeling I just don't recognise in myself when I look at him and even more when I then look at her. It's absolute awe. I glance to the ceiling and pull in a steadying breath.

'Oh!' Talia all but squeals.

'What?' I whip to look at her but she's staring in rapture at Lukas.

'He's smiling!' she says.

She's smiling too and she's beautiful and now I don't know where to look. I'm torn between the two of them.

'And?' I mutter weakly.

'He hasn't smiled before. This is his first smile.'

'Really?' I look back at Lukas then back at her and back again, and again.

'First social smile.' She nods. 'Happens between eight and twelve weeks and here he is…smiling at you.'

There are tears in her eyes and she's so effervescent there's no way she's faking this. I talk more nonsense to

Lukas because it just bubbles out of me and he smiles again and Talia *beams*.

A chuckle escapes me. I want to do anything. Everything. I feel utterly alive—I want to keep them both with me and have them happy but in the same breath I feel a sudden helpless futility. Because this is something I can't ensure. I couldn't help my parents' happiness. Nor my grandfather's. I don't think I can do happy families. It goes wrong—it never lasts.

But I'm beginning to get her. She's done everything for herself—and her sister—for years. She's so determinedly independent I know the reasons why she doesn't want to rely on anyone are deep-seated. She's been let down before.

So I'll try to do whatever it takes to make sure she can't walk out on me again. Because I want this to work for Lukas. Somehow I need her to trust me. I need her to talk to me. Talia's withholding of information wasn't just about protecting Ava. It was about protecting herself too. Because people are selfish. They do things for their own reasons. Me included.

We sit together on the floor. Lukas is stretched out between us and we each have a toy in hand—waving them in front of him to tease another smile. The rabbit I'm holding is old. One of its ears is at risk of spontaneously severing. Possibly its head too. It's surprisingly easy to sit here with her. It reminds me of those tragic jokes we shared when we were in the gondola.

'Do you have siblings?' she suddenly asks.

'Time to swap life stories?' I shoot her a sardonic look.

Her shoulder lifts—half apology, half amusement.

'No siblings,' I mutter. 'For a while I wished I had them, then I was glad I didn't.'

'Because your parents fought?'

I nod. 'They used me.' I was alternately a weapon or a prize. 'Any sibling would have been an adversary. We'd have been played off against each other.'

She dangles her toy above Lukas. 'It was that bad?'

'Worse.'

'I was lucky to have Ava…' She sighs deeply and her worried expression make me tense.

It's obvious she has more to say but she's gone silent. I fake patience and waggle the ripped-up rabbit at Lukas. I should win an acting award, I really should.

'About Ava…'

I wait.

'I want her to believe I'm happy. That I want this.'

'You mean move to Australia with me?' There's a hit in there that makes my chest ache.

She puffs out a breath. 'I don't want her to doubt…'

'You want us to act like we're happy together. Is that what you mean?'

'Yes.' She swallows. 'I don't want her to worry about me.'

She's spent her life caring for her sister. Maybe her sister should have been more aware of how hard her big sister was working for her. But Talia wasn't honest even then.

It's a good reminder that she's a liar. She lies to the people who should be closest to her. I know how much that hurts the one lied to. Supposedly *protected*.

I almost tear the ear off the rabbit. I slide it into my pocket so Talia doesn't see. 'You want me to act the besotted boyfriend?'

She must have caught the anger in my expression because she turns away. 'Forget it.'

I reach out and turn her back. I run my hand through her hair and see that smokiness enter her eyes. Is *this* honest,

Talia? I ignore her words and focus on the micro actions of her body that she can't control. The flush that builds in her cheeks. The quickening breath. The way she leans a bit close without even realising. I lean closer and she mirrors me so we're almost intimate, our baby content between us.

'Trust me,' I say softly. 'She'll understand what it is you *really* want.'

CHAPTER ELEVEN

Talia

THE NEXT MORNING we're driven to Dunedin in that fancy car with the so-silent-he's-almost-robotic driver. As every kilometre passes I get more nervous. This is crazy precarious. I desperately want to see Ava before leaving but I've no idea how I'm going to explain everything.

'She doesn't need to know we've been…'

Out of touch? Estranged? I can't even figure out how to talk about this to him, let alone my younger sister, who I've tried to be a solid support to.

Dain doesn't lift his gaze from the laptop he's typing on. 'It'll be fine.'

I knock on her door and wait while holding Lukas in my arms. I've an almost violent urge to run away—I don't want Ava to feel as if I've let her down in some way. As if I've made Mum's mistakes all over again. Dain slings a heavy arm around my shoulders, literally anchoring me in place as if he senses my urge to flee. He steps in close and almost presses me into his side as if sheltering me and Lukas from a cold wind.

'Stop worrying.'

His breath warms the side of my neck and I shiver and

he cuddles me closer still. His heat seeps through my old down jacket and the anxiety inside morphs into something else. I look at Lukas in my arms to hide the sudden emotion sweeping through me. The door opens.

'Talia?' It's a stage whisper at first, then Ava's voice rises twenty decibels. *'Talia?'*

She stares from me to Lukas in my arms then up to Dain, standing tall beside me, then back to me and around the three of us again—a circle of movement and amazement.

'Surprise...' I say weakly.

'Oh, my...' Ava looks from Lukas then up at Dain again. 'Oh, *my*!'

'May we come in?' He floors her with his most charming smile.

Gaping, Ava steps back and we file inside her cramped student flat.

'You've been keeping secrets,' she hisses at me.

'I know. This is Lukas.' I pass my baby to his aunt. 'And his father, Dain.'

Ava melts as she stares down at Lukas. 'Talia, he's gorgeous.'

Yep, both of them.

'How did you—when?' Ava's eyes fill with curiosity and reproach. 'What's been going on?'

Emotion clogs my throat. At the sight of her displeasure I suddenly feel so guilty. I hadn't really thought this might hurt her.

'Talia didn't want to worry you,' Dain says gently.

'I met Dain in Queenstown,' I say. 'One thing led to another...'

'Sure did.' Ava smiles awkwardly.

'It was an instant thing,' Dain says.

He still has his arm around me. He's playing a part. I

play my part too. Only for me it isn't a pretence. My legs really are like jelly, my heart isn't just racing, it's turbulent. The attraction that hit me the moment I first saw him rears from its slumber. But it's always been there. It never left me and now it's wide, wide awake.

Ava offers us tea or coffee and apologises for the tiny flat. I'm used to it but I see Dain's assessing glance around and stiffen. He sees me notice him and simply holds me closer. And that just makes me flustered.

'You look thinner in the face.' Ava studies me intently. 'Are you sure you're okay?'

I feel Dain's quick frowning look down. After what happened last night I don't need him being any more over-protective. 'It's just been busy. I'm fine.'

'You're able to feed him okay?' Ava checks.

'He's a hungry boy.'

'So you need to be eating enough to—'

'Stop it.' I force a laugh. 'You're a second-year med student, not a paediatrician already.'

'Maternal nutrition is—'

'Enough. I eat well.' I shush her. 'Dain's overprotective enough, you'll only make him worse.'

'Good.' Ava shoots him an imperious look. 'Make sure she eats properly. Little and often.' Ava glances at me again. 'Make that *lots* and often.'

I shake my head.

'You work too hard. You always have.' Ava leans close and her voice lowers. 'You should have told me.'

I feel queasy at her plaintive tone. I've hurt her when it was the last thing I wanted.

'You needed to focus on your studies,' I murmur.

I feel Dain tense beside me and I quickly glance at him.

'You've been sending me money all this time.' Ava suddenly clicks. 'Did you work all through your pregnancy?'

'Lukas was a little unexpected.' Dain steps in and fills the sharpening silence. 'I'm here to support both him and Talia now.'

The frown in Ava's eyes doesn't fade. 'You think you can get Talia to depend on you? She doesn't let *anyone* in.'

Ava blinks and her head swivels towards me. Dain watches me too and I feel as though I've let them both down. I'm weak and I go for the distraction he provides.

'Ava,' I say gently. 'Dain's helping with your fees now.'

'What?'

'Have you checked your banking app lately?' I ask.

Ava winces. 'Why would I—?'

'Have a look at it,' Dain suggests.

Ava passes Lukas back to me and pulls out her phone. Her face goes all blotchy when she opens her app.

'My accountant will be in touch,' Dain says quietly. 'There might be some tax implications, but she'll manage that for you.'

'Are you for real?' Ava looks at Dain and then at me. 'Is this for *real*?' She shakes her head vigorously. 'I can't accept this from a stranger. I *can't*—'

'You can accept this from *family*,' Dain interrupts firmly. 'And that's what we are now. Right, Talia?'

I've lost the power of speech. I'm still clamped to his side and he drops a kiss on the top of my head. It brings *everything* back—the scent of him, the strength of him, the sheer vitality of him that's so bewitching. I liquefy inside.

Ava's stunned to silence as well. Yep. Full Dain Anzelotti effect in action.

She looks at me. I feel the heat on my skin and know I'm blushing. I can't hide my response to him.

'Consider it a scholarship,' he says. 'You've accepted those before, right?'

Ava nods but she doesn't take her eyes off me. I'm trembling inside and I hold Lukas more carefully because I have to direct my energy somewhere.

Dain smiles but both his arms are around me now as if he knows I'm close to spontaneously combusting and he's literally holding me together.

Ava's eyes soften. 'Oh, Talia,' she whispers. 'I'm so pleased for you.'

She isn't talking about the money. What she sees—or what she *thinks* she sees—is wonderful. It's what I ache for. And what I don't have. She believes the lie he's presenting, only right now it's truth for me—I'm in thrall to him and I absolutely want to go with him to wherever he chooses…

'I'm taking Talia and Lukas to Australia.' Dain's voice is gravelly.

'Australia?'

'Dain has a family home there,' I explain as Ava's eyes go huge. I've no idea if that's actually true but I know the impact the idea will have on Ava—the same impact it has on me. 'It'll be Lukas's family home too.'

Ava nods slowly. 'And yours. A permanent place to stay.' She sends me a small smile. 'Finally.' Ava blinks rapidly and looks down at Lukas. 'I can't believe I'm an aunty.' She breathes in shakily. 'I'm going to miss him and I barely know him.'

I glance up at Dain. There's a bleak expression in his eyes that he quickly blinks away when he catches my eye.

'We'll send lots of photos. Videos. Calls.' He turns his attention to Ava and promises.

He never got those. I never *sent* any—not after that one shot of Lukas as a newborn. I feel terrible. 'We really need to go now, Ava, I'm sorry. We have to get to the airport. Can't miss the flight.'

'Ava's like you,' Dain says bluntly as we pull away from the kerb. 'Bossy, untrusting.' He sighs. 'We didn't get far in the life-story swap yesterday. What happened with your dad?'

I shoot him a look. 'He walked out when I was eight and Ava was four. There were always other women and once he'd left for good he didn't want to know us at all. He just wasn't interested.' I grit my teeth. 'My mother didn't cope. She thought she needed someone, so she went from one jerk to the next. She had high hopes for every new guy she let into her life and when those hopes were shattered, we moved. Every time.'

'How many times?'

I shrug. 'I can't remember exactly.'

'Every year?'

'At least.'

His expression tightens. 'And you took care of Ava.'

I swallow. 'Of course. Now you've met her, you know why. She's wonderful.'

It only takes minutes to get to the airport but we don't head to the main terminal, but to a smaller building to the side. The driver and an equally discreet porter gather our belongings from the car while Dain lifts Lukas out as though he's been doing it for months. Yep, he's a fast learner. And even though we've left Ava and there's no need for any further pretence, Dain doesn't distance himself any. He wraps an arm around me and hustles me to a small counter, shielding me and Lukas from the few other people in the room.

'Are we leaving right away?' I mutter.

I'm more nervous now than I was about seeing Ava and it's not the actual flight putting the fear in me.

'You don't want to?'

'I wouldn't mind some lunch,' I prevaricate.

Because I'm about to be cooped up in a very small space with him for *hours* and I don't think I can trust myself. I don't even step away from him now when I actually can. Pretending for Ava has stirred me up—I can't help wishing that the tenderness in his touch were true.

'We'll eat on board,' he says.

That's when I glance out of the window and see the plane on the tarmac. It's sleek and has no commercial markings. The truth dawns on me. 'You have a *private* jet?'

'We would've flown to Dunedin from Queenstown, but the pilot went to pick up your passports. He's just finalising the flight plan for us now.'

My lungs seem to shrink. I'd forgotten about the passports. But they're here—turned around super quick because of his power and resources. 'You always travel on your own jet?'

'I like the privacy it gives me,' he says.

'Because you're secretive?' Maybe he doesn't want anyone to see Lukas and me with him—maybe that's why he's hurrying us out onto the tarmac.

'Not *secretive*,' he says coolly, guiding me towards the stairs. 'Private. There's a difference.'

CHAPTER TWELVE

Dain

I PAUSE, HOLDING Lukas as Talia regards the jet even more warily the nearer we get to it.

'Is it big enough to get us all the way?' she asks, drawing in a shuddering breath.

'I promise I'll get you all the way,' I mutter with a smirk. Yes, I'm all but waggling my eyebrows with the innuendo. I can't help myself.

She looks at me and the colour rises in her cheeks.

Yeah. I've spent the morning right beside her. Touching her. I've been inhaling her scent and feeling the warmth of her soft skin and all I want is to strip her and stroke her until she's slippery and supple and hot enough to take all of *me* again. I still want her and I can't hide it. The way she melted against me earlier tells me she's the same. That part of the pretence in front of Ava was no pretence at all. She still wants me too. But the complications—Lukas's well-being—are too much.

'I meant is it big enough to get us all the way to Australia?' she clarifies primly.

'It got me here.' I smile. 'You don't feel safe?'

'I never feel safe. Not entirely. I don't think it's possible to.'

My gut clenches. She's spent her life worrying the rug was about to be tugged from beneath her and it seems it happened time and time again. So no wonder she fights for control and is so determined to do everything herself. She's always had to. She never lets other people help—or not much at any rate, which infuriates me, even though I've learned she's been let down by the people she should have been able to trust most. Her parents. And that's something I can well understand.

'It's worse now Lukas is here.' She glances at the plane again. 'I'm horribly overprotective.'

Yeah, I know the feeling. 'I guess that's pretty normal,' I mutter as I glance down at him in my arms. 'He's utterly defenceless. He doesn't just need protection, he needs everything. He's completely reliant on you for survival.'

'On *us*,' she says softly.

Right. I have to pause for a moment as warmth bursts in my chest as if a damned firework's been ignited in there. That's the first indicator from her that we're a team and in this together. And even though she's the one who's prevented this, that she now acknowledges it brings a burn of satisfaction to me.

We board and strap in. There's a cot for Lukas but for take-off I place him in her lap and she uses a baby belt that's attached to hers. Despite what she's acknowledged, I know better than to offer to take him for this moment. I know she can't give him over to me yet. But I can be there for them both. Her face pales but I suspect that it's not just the flight bothering her but the enormity of this action. I don't dismiss how hard this has to be for her.

Once we're settled I reach across and take her hand in

mine. She closes her eyes but doesn't pull away. I know she doesn't want to need me, but that she takes my touch soothes something inside me. I can't resist leaning closer on the pretext of looking at Lukas. Although I want to look at him too. As the plane accelerates down the runway her hand twists and she holds me back. Tightly. An electrical pulse charges between us and the only response I'm capable of is to hold her even more tightly. A shiver runs through her and she opens her eyes and looks straight into mine. Hers are an even deeper brown than usual and I don't think that emotion is fear.

It takes everything not to lean in and kiss her. Yet despite that keen frustration victory hums in my veins. Our physical compatibility is undeniable and right now I feel like a damned saint. I've been living like a monk for months. So not me. I work hard. I like reward. I like knowing I can get what I want. Her smile is what I want and her body is next on the menu.

Except it can't be. There's Lukas. There's all this complication.

I release my seat belt as soon as we've levelled out, and pull together a snack plate for her. Keeping myself busy is the only way I can get through this.

I take Lukas from her and settle him into the cot that's been installed in the plane. The cabin door is locked. I told the flight crew not to disturb us when we first boarded. I pass her the papers I printed early this morning before leaving the holiday home in Queenstown.

'Will you look through these résumés and let me know if you have a preference?' I ask. 'I'll arrange interviews for the top three as soon as we land.'

She looks confused. 'For what position?'

'I have a cleaner and a team who come and look after

the grounds as well as a chef who's onsite for some of the week and leaves meals for the weekends. But this is the first nanny I've had to employ and I assumed you'd want to have input into that decision.'

'You want Lukas to have a nanny?' She's arctic and there's no way she'd take my hand now.

But I expected a spiky response from Ms I-Don't-Need-Anything-From-Anyone.

'You worked right through your pregnancy and continued the moment you left hospital after giving birth,' I point out calmly. 'You need a break. Lukas needs you to have a break. To sleep.'

'I don't need a break.'

'The dark circles under your eyes tell a different story.'

Her back straightens. Yep, just made her spikier. Too bad.

'The nanny isn't making any major parenting decisions.' I aim to inject a little levity. 'It's enough that the two of us will probably debate them intensely. I've no doubt we'll overthink our way around all sides of any issue and won't need any outside interference to make it worse.'

She shoots me a look but to my pleasure she can't hold her smile for long. She actually chuckles. 'I don't *want* to disagree with you.'

'Then don't,' I reply, as if it's the most obvious answer ever. But I feel a ridiculous level of relief and I smile back at her. 'You can't do it all by yourself, all of the time. You don't have to. Not any more. You can share the load.'

'Like you do?'

'I have plenty of people who support me—I just told you only a few of my home team. So let's get a nanny to tend to him for the late night feed. Just that one. We'll see how it goes and then assess. Okay?'

She doesn't actually know I'm being uncharacteristically reasonable here so she can't appreciate my effort in that regard.

'Okay,' she mumbles. 'Thank you.'

I can't resist teasing her more so I lean really close. 'Pardon? I didn't quite catch that.'

'Thank you.' But there's a defiant gleam in her eye as if giving me thanks is the last thing she wants to do.

And yeah, it's the last thing I want from her. I *do* want her time and attention. Her company. But somehow that has to be separate from all this and I can't see how that's possible so I pull back.

The flight drags. She reads every résumé cover to cover and puts them in an ordered pile of preference. Then she plays on her phone. I'm actually fidgeting because I want to talk to her but at the same time I want to control that urge. Just to prove to myself that I can. She suddenly reaches over and offers her phone. The screen is unlocked and there's a photo of Lukas in front of me.

'I thought…' She shrugs and worries her lip somewhat helplessly. 'I don't know if you want to see them but, if you flick through, there's every photo or little film I have of Lukas since he was born.'

Speechless, I take the phone from her and stare hungrily at the screen. I don't know how much time passes as I absorb every image, every small video, every glimpse into his little life thus far. He's only three months old but she has a hundred pictures of him and every last one is stunning. Maybe it's her social media work but the woman can construct a frame. Maybe it's that her subject is so completely perfect. He's so beautiful. Yeah, I'm smitten with him. I never imagined I could feel so much for something—someone—so small. I slowly scroll backwards through the pictures and at one I draw a sharp breath. It doesn't show Lukas. It's Talia. A very heavily pregnant Talia.

Talia glances across and leans over to see which picture has me so floored.

'Oh.' Her cheeks redden. 'Romy took some. She said I needed to record the pregnancy because it goes fast. So I posed a few times.'

She's looking embarrassed in the photo and even more embarrassed now. My heart pounds. I swipe back one more.

'Oh!' She gasps. The colour in her face instantly intensifies. 'That's terrible,' she babbles. 'I forgot it was there. I didn't mean...'

I don't let her take the phone back. It's a bathroom selfie. She's wearing a bra and panties and nothing else. She has to be almost at full term. She's so beautiful my heart basically bursts.

I just stare at it. At her. Raw yearning overwhelms me. 'I missed your *entire* pregnancy,' I mutter between gritted teeth. 'I never got to *see* you...not once...'

Not that night in the gondola cabin either. It was too dark. There were only glimpses of perfection when lightning lit the sky. And right now I'm almost overcome by the urge to tumble her to the floor and impregnate her again here and now and then chain her to me so I don't miss another damned second of it. Yeah. Shocking.

I don't, of course. But I do tap the phone and flag all the photos I've just been looking at.

'What are you doing?' she mumbles.

'I want a copy of them,' I almost growl as I pull out my own phone and wirelessly transfer the files. 'Okay?'

I'm too gruff and it's not really a question because I really don't want her to say no. And for a guy who—I fully admit—is fully paranoid about other people having photos of me, it's rough of me to just send copies of these direct to my phone.

'Even those ones?'

Yeah. The ones of her. I nod jerkily. There's silence and I slowly look up. I have to look her in the eyes to check I have her consent. Her bloody beautiful deep brown eyes snare me. I just drown in them. She's still for a while, not saying anything while she reads who knows what in my own tense expression.

'Okay,' she says softly.

I swallow and make myself build some humanity. 'Tell me about his birth,' I croak. 'Was it okay?'

She hesitates and now her gaze skitters from mine. 'I don't remember a lot of it.'

Liar. She's holding back from me. And suddenly I'm furious with her. I want to find out more. Disappointment merges with challenge. I want the entire truth from her. And that's when I accept I'm willing to do whatever it takes to get it.

CHAPTER THIRTEEN

Talia

I CAN'T HOLD his gaze. He's missed so much and I feel terrible. I should have pushed harder. Showing him the photos was a peace offering, the smallest of ways in which I could try to make amends. But I don't tell him about Lukas's delivery even though I should. I don't want him getting angry with me for going through that alone and I suspect he will. For a moment here on the plane things were good between us—we even laughed. Now there's a flash of that bleakness in his gaze as I pass off the question, but he says nothing. He holds my phone back out to me.

'Now you have my number,' he says dryly. 'No excuse not to stay in touch.'

As I take my phone the plane shudders. I stiffen. Before I can breathe his hand is on mine.

'It's just a few bumps. Give it a moment.'

Sure enough the plane settles as we zoom through the clouds but my pulse races on regardless. He hasn't released my hand and I haven't tried to pull away.

'What is it with you needing a comforting touch in life-threatening situations?' he teases.

'I think that's a pretty normal human response.' I bluff

but it's nice to see his smile again. 'And you're the one who grabbed *my* hand.'

He chuckles. 'You're a good liar.'

I shoot him a startled look.

'You lied to Ava very easily about us,' he elaborates.

I press my lips together. 'Only because I didn't want her to worry at all. Not ever.'

'I guessed that was why.' He sighs. 'But it makes me wonder who you do ever open up to.'

I shoot him another startled look and pull my hand free of his. He doesn't try to stop me.

His low bitter laugh mocks me. 'Yeah, no one. I figured that.'

I'm irritated because I'm certain *he* doesn't open up to anyone either. 'And your point?'

He straightens in his seat and leans closer. 'I don't want you to lie to me. Not ever.'

He echoes my words. I swallow because while it could be considered a threat it's more of a warm invitation and it's utterly disarming.

'I'd like you to promise me that you won't,' he adds steadily. 'And don't hold back on all the truth either.'

Yeah, he knows I omit things. Because I just have and of course he knows it. But it's for good reason—or so I've always thought.

'I think you owe me that,' he finishes.

I realise the photos weren't enough. Nor was the apology. He needs the whole truth. He's done all the right things since finding out about Lukas. He's tried to give me time, space, he's taken me to see Ava and offered unquestioning support. I haven't. I need to be honest with him.

Not making more of an effort to tell him about Lukas was terrible. It's as though a fog has lifted from my mind.

For me to hold his lifestyle against him—to be so *judgemental*—was wrong. I need to course correct. Now.

'You know that night at the gondola was out of character for me.' My throat clogs because this is personal and it's hard to say.

His eyes widen and he slowly nods. 'Yet you assume it wasn't out of character for me also?' His focus is even more intense now. 'What do you think you know about me?'

I bite my lip, embarrassed because I've been emotional. He wants to be there for Lukas. He wants to make everything work between us. He's trying. So I need to try too. I need to be honest even if it means more anger from him.

'I found a photo of you with another woman taken later on the night we were together.' The thought of it still turns my stomach. Was she his girlfriend? I hate to think I was the other woman in a cheating situation.

He sits up straight. 'You what?'

'I know you met up with another woman that night.' I hurry to tell him I know the truth. 'It's your prerogative, I guess, it's not like we were—'

'You—'

'Allowed my own prejudice to cloud my thinking,' I interrupt him because I need to get all this said before I chicken out. 'I made assumptions and I was wrong to and I'm sorry. And the thing is—if I'm really honest with myself it's not because I was being judgemental of your lifestyle. But rather I was jealous.'

His jaw drops. 'Of this other woman?'

'No.' I swallow. 'Of you.'

He looks mystified. 'For...'

'Having fun?' I shrug and finish weakly. It's so stupid and I've made bad decisions because of it.

I assumed he wouldn't be interested in being a father.

None of the cheats my mother dated ever were. My own cheat of a father sure wasn't. I tarnished Dain with their brush.

He stares at me for a moment. I can't read his reaction as he rubs his mouth with his fingers.

'Show me the photo,' he suddenly orders.

'I can't. I don't have it.'

'There's Wi-Fi on the plane, search for it again and show me.' He's very businesslike.

Yep, instant regrets on being so honest. But I do as he asks.

'There are almost no photos of me online,' he says conversationally as I fumble with my phone. 'I have a team who keep it that way. That's partly why it was all but impossible for you to get in touch with me directly.'

Because he's a control freak who hates being in the press. Yep, I've got that. And I don't blame him now I know a little more about his parents putting him on the front page in their personal fight.

But it's the Internet and some things never die on the Internet. I find the picture and turn it so he can see. It was in a gossip-column piece from a small Queenstown paper that I followed on my social media. It popped up in my feed the morning after that momentous night. The photo showed him with a famous New Zealand model and I was appalled.

'I'm not identified in the caption,' he says thoughtfully. 'That must be why my minions didn't pick it up.'

'But it's *you*.' I brace as he studies the photo. He doesn't deny it.

'Is she your girlfriend?' I ask.

The corners of his mouth twitch. 'What makes you think we're *together*?'

Well, duh, you only need to look at the way the model

is looking at *him* to know they're intimate. But Dain's eyebrows are raised questioningly and I can't tell him it's all in her eyes.

'We're not even holding hands,' he points out calmly. 'Not kissing. Not touching at all.'

I swallow. 'Because you're private.'

That he isn't named in that caption actually speaks to the power of his discretion. Maybe the photographer didn't recognise him and was interested in the model.

He regards me steadily. 'Okay, I'll give you that.'

So he was with her. My innards shrivel.

'But you didn't notice my hair apparently grew about three inches in less than a couple hours?' He watches me.

'What?' I stare at him then back at the photo.

'My hair was shorter when I was with you,' he says. 'Don't you remember tugging on it? Because I remember you tugging on it.'

A flame of heat rivers through me. With trembling fingers I study that photo again.

He's right, I didn't look too closely at the time because I was cringing—and I was too busy feeling inadequate looking at her. But now I do look more closely. And, yes, his hair is longer than it was that night.

'This photo was taken two years ago when I met Willow. I haven't seen her since then, though according to that caption she was back in Queenstown that weekend. But I never saw her and last I heard she was modelling in Paris.'

Willow is even more famous than he is. The gossip piece focused on her, not the man escorting her. And she suits the name, what with her endless limbs and, oh, yes, I am jealous. I clocked the location—a cool bar in Queenstown—and, given the date of the article, I assumed the photo was

taken that night. That he went from a quick canapé—me—
to the sumptuous feast that was her.

'So she wasn't your girlfriend?' I ask.

'Not the night we were together,' he says. 'I don't cheat.'

Now I feel even worse.

But Dain actually chuckles. 'You really screwed up.'

I really did.

He inhales. 'As penance I think you ought to be wholly
honest with me.'

I glance up at him, confused. I've just confessed the
worst.

'Were you a virgin that night?' he asks bluntly.

I shrivel—emotionally that is. If only I could *really*
shrivel right out of existence. How did he know? Did he
guess? I'm mortified. 'I...'

Can't even breathe the words.

But he just waits.

'Why does it matter?' I mumble as I eventually nod.

'Why didn't you tell me then?'

I swallow.

'You couldn't, right?' he says. 'You couldn't be that vulnerable.'

'I've never regretted it. Not for a moment,' I reassure him
in an embarrassed rush. 'It was amazing. You were...' I trail
off and look at him. 'Are you even more angry with me?'

'I'm feeling all kinds of things about you, Talia. But
yeah, anger is one of them.' He looks thoughtful. 'And
you're jealous of my supposed lifestyle?'

My lips are suddenly dry and I lick them. 'Do you deny
your lifestyle is...uh...exciting?'

'I don't think it's as extensive as what you're thinking.'
He looks right into my eyes.

I don't want to think about it too closely. 'Oh?'

His gaze is unwavering. 'I haven't had sex in about a year.'

My jaw drops. 'You mean...?'

No. Surely not.

He closes my mouth with a finger beneath my chin. 'Yeah. I do mean.' His gaze deepens. 'Let me guess, you don't believe me.'

'I...' *Am floored.*

'Yet it's *true*,' he says and he's somehow even closer.

'Why didn't you?' I blurt.

'Why didn't you?'

I can't answer.

'Here's the thing, Talia,' he says slowly. 'I won't lie to you either. If nothing else there has to be absolute honesty between us because we have to work together. For Lukas. So honesty always. Deal?'

I'm bamboozled by his revelation but I hear that caveat—*if nothing else.*

'Deal,' I breathe.

He doesn't look satisfied. In fact his expression tightens and he's somehow closer.

'You've worked hard to care for your sister for a long time. Worked hard to care for Lukas,' he says almost thoughtfully. 'You've never let anyone take care of your needs—not until that night with me, right?'

I can only stare at him.

'And not since then?' His sudden smile is saturnine. 'You should be indulged, Talia.'

'I should.' My spellbound agreement slides out on a whisper.

I can't turn away from him. I can't look away from the heat in his blue, blue eyes. I can't ignore this desire any more. I'm utterly still as he slowly moves closer. His smile is all I can see. His touch is all I want. And at last he's there—his mouth is on mine. I open to him on a moan and he echoes it with one of his own. The pressure is hot and escalates in seconds. I clutch his shoulders. I thought I'd remembered but I was wrong. This intensity shuts my mind down. I just want him. All of him. Here. Now.

He growls in the back of his throat and I feel his muscles bunch. He drags me across his lap and I tremble in absolute rapture at being in his arms again. I press against him and the kisses deepen. He teases me with his tongue. His hands hold me—hard and secure—and sweep down my body. I'm aching and ecstatic and I just pour it all into kissing him and lose myself in the bliss.

I pay no attention to the voice saying something from far away.

But suddenly Dain tears his mouth from mine. With a muttered swearword he lifts me back into my seat. Dazed, I can only look at him in confusion—and yearning.

'That was the captain speaking.' He half laughs, half groans. 'Seat belt on.' He fastens my belt before tending to Lukas. 'We're landing.'

But I'm still up in the clouds and I really don't want to return to earth.

CHAPTER FOURTEEN

Dain

IT WASN'T SUPPOSED to happen. I intended to do whatever it took to get her to trust me but also keep my damned distance. But somehow she's defused my temper and the damned endless lust I have for her has me so distracted I can't catch my breath. But she wants me just as much. Right back. And I'm all but feral inside.

We land in Brisbane and I dispense with my waiting chauffeur to drive Talia and Lukas to my house myself. I don't want my off-balance state to be obvious to everyone. Frankly I've yet to figure how I'm going to introduce them to my staff, how I'm going to explain their sudden appearance in my life to anyone. But it doesn't matter, I can delay most of that. Right now I just want to be alone with them both.

'This is a beautiful area...' She's wide-eyed as she looks at the leafy neighbourhood I begin to slow down in. 'You don't live in one of your own apartments?'

'When working in Sydney or Melbourne, sure. But this is my place to escape and I thought it would be a better place to bring Lukas. It offers total privacy.'

'It's huge.' She's pale as we drive through the massive security gates. 'How do you manage it?'

'I have staff.' I pull up outside the house and pause, not understanding her wariness. 'You don't like it?' That I care so much about her opinion is just weird.

'Oh, no, it's amazing. It's just really huge.'

'With this space and privacy I can fully relax. Property is work. This isn't work. This is my paradise.' I get out of the car and breathe in the perfumed scent of the garden. Then I shrug. 'Like you, I moved a lot when I was a kid. I was shuttled from apartment to apartment and always being asked to compare them—which was bigger, which was better. I just wanted to stay in the one place and not have to decide and try to placate them. So this is wish fulfilment perhaps.'

'It's your *home*,' she mutters.

'Right.' I feel awkward. 'A garden and a pool and I can have my friends over to play without worrying World War Three is about to erupt in front of them.'

She smiles at that. 'You have your friends over often?'

Her smile pulls my own and I start to relax. 'I've been known to have parties.'

'Debauched dance parties with beautiful women?'

'That's what you immediately picture?' My mood lightens more and I laugh. 'You see me and think sexy dancing?'

She blushes delightfully. My smile just gets bigger and I'm half tempted to dance towards her right now. Her inexperience and unexplored desire and passionate curiosity intrigue me. Because I also know she's an extremist—it's evident in the hours she works, the lengths she goes to— misguidedly sometimes—to look after those she loves. She's either all in or she's all out.

In some respects I'm the same. Physically I want all

in. But while the chemistry between us crackles I'm wary about dealing with it. Usually sex is uncomplicated. Desire is transient. Once it's sated I move on and I've stayed on good terms with many of the women I've slept with. Because emotional boundaries don't get crossed. I make sure there are no expectations, offer no 'relationship'—I've no interest in that burden. Because it is a burden.

So surely I could sleep with her again and us remain pleasant in parenting Lukas? The problem is she's untrusting too. She's been hurt by her past and I can't be sure she wouldn't turn and try to block me out once we're done. I never want Lukas to witness a war like that of my parents.

I think Talia believes in happy families as little as I do. So I've got to resist the temptation to touch her. We'll keep things calm and serene and safe. I'll never make her some impossible-to-keep promise. Because the only thing I'm certain of is the impermanence of any affair.

I step forward and lift Lukas from the car, carrying him while I take Talia on a quick tour.

'The parties are purely for business,' I explain. 'I need to be engaged with the community—keep the profile up. So there are charity balls, philanthropic events.' I can't resist walking near enough for our shoulders to brush. 'The beautiful and the wealthy attend. Future and current clients.'

To be honest I probably should have one soon. It's been a while since I have and it would be a way of revealing Talia and Lukas are in my life—at least to those I work most closely with. They're better off being informed directly by me rather than by the inevitable whisperings and speculation that will begin. But it doesn't have to happen this weekend or anything. We all need to settle in together first.

I lead her through the atrium and into the first of the

living areas—the one with the view over the pool and tennis court.

'Do you play tennis? Swim?' I ask. 'There's a home gym, yoga room and sauna as well. Use any of them any time.' I want her to feel comfortable here. 'There's a home cinema too—'

'You have everything you could ever want.' She doesn't look comfortable. 'You never need to leave the place if you don't want to.'

'Right.' I tense a little. Because yeah, that was part of it. Full privacy.

'You know I want to keep working,' she says in a low voice.

'I know.' I inhale deeply. At that comment I can't wait any longer and can only hope my assistants have been as efficient as they usually are. 'On that, I have something to show you in the pool room.'

She shoots me a wary glance. I'm actually nervous, which is ridiculous. Still carrying Lukas, I walk past the tennis court and the pool to the low building at the back.

'This is the pool room,' I explain.

'It's a whole other *house*.'

I smile because that's actually true. It's a three-bedroom cottage.

'Do you want me to live in here rather than the main house?' she asks.

A flash of guilt makes me flinch. When I first thought about her moving here I considered that, but now there's no way. 'I think we both need to be near Lukas at night and he'll definitely be in the main house.'

I lead her to the large kitchen usually reserved for pizza parties and pool refreshments and let her walk in ahead of me.

'I've had my assistant set a few things up, but you can change the layout and of course you can exchange any items if there's another brand of equipment that you prefer.'

'Are you kidding me?' Her eyes are huge as she slowly turns on the spot.

I lean against the doorjamb and feel a smug satisfaction for the first time in days. I've shocked—and pleased—her. It feels good. I want to please her some more. I want to see her smile and her skin flush and hear her light laughter.

She runs her hand lightly over the gleaming chrome of the brand-new Italian espresso machine. It's a commercial one with so many levers I wouldn't know where to start, but she clearly does because she whispers its name beneath her breath with the reverence of meeting a deity. Watching her makes me smile harder.

Then she sees the double camera set-up—the rotating mount so she can film directly above the polished counter-top and get that bird's eye view, and the other camera on a free-standing tripod. There are diffusers and other technical gear so she can get the exact lighting she needs. There are smaller boxes that I told my staff to leave unopened because I thought she might like to enjoy unwrapping them herself—it's crockery and tools for any kind of coffee shoot she can think of. She's speechless but that doesn't mean I can't read her mind on this.

'I know your channel is important to you,' I say. 'This way you can keep making content while being here at home with Lukas. It will do for now, right?'

Her wide-eyed gaze turns troubled. 'You hate social media.'

'Well, I didn't think *I'd* be in your videos.' I smile at her.

'Right.' She almost smiles back but then she goes solemn again. 'I'll pay you back.'

I instantly chill. That's not a conversation that interests me, but I don't want to argue with her. I turn and begin walking back to the main house. 'I'll show you the nursery and your room now.'

She runs to catch me and grabs my shoulder to make me stop. 'Thank you, Dain.'

I stare down at her. Yeah, I wanted to please her but oddly I really don't want her gratitude. I don't want her feeling beholden to me. I want there to be nothing like that between us again.

'No problem.' I'm gruff. 'Keeping you happy is important.'

She pulls back and I want to bite out my tongue even though what I've said is true.

I keep moving. I show her through the airy bedroom suites that have been arranged for them. There's a room for Lukas. One for a nanny next door while Talia's is further along. My bedroom is at the other end of the corridor but I don't make the mistake of showing her right inside that—my self-control has its limits.

'I need to do some work,' I say shortly once I've swiftly nodded whose is whose room. 'Will you settle Lukas into the nursery?'

'Of course, he's due for a snack.'

I carefully hand our son to her. It's torture being so close and getting a hit of her soft fragrance. I'm tempted to go into the nursery with her and sit with them while she tends to our baby. Except I need to get my head back together and I haven't done any real work in days.

Only half an hour later I can't stay away any longer. I go back to the nursery half expecting to see them both taking a nap. But while Lukas is bundled up fast asleep in his crib, Talia isn't there. I hear noises and walk along the corridor. Talia's in her bedroom—red-faced and frantic and rummaging through her bags.

'What's wrong?' I watch her tearing through her few clothes. 'You've lost something?'

'A toy Romy gave to Lukas.' She tips one bag upside down and keeps shaking it even though there's clearly nothing else to fall from it. 'I can't find it. It isn't anywhere. But I was sure I'd packed it.'

Her whisper is urgent and upset.

I freeze. 'Are you talking about that ripped-up rabbit?'

'Yes.' She whips her head up. 'Have you seen it?'

'It was almost decapitated—'

'I hadn't had time to fix it.' She's suddenly in a fury. 'You *took* it?'

CHAPTER FIFTEEN

Talia

'IT WASN'T YOURS to take.' Anger surges into me. 'What did you do with it?'

He's frozen. 'Talia—'

'You got rid of it? Threw it out?' I gape at him in horror. 'Because it was ragged?'

He walks out of the room and I'm so furious I follow him, not stopping to see where he's going, not stopping my tirade. He doesn't want to deal with my emotion? Too bad. 'Wasn't it good enough for your standards? Didn't it fit into this perfect nursery you've put together like magic?'

It was broken and it wasn't perfect but it was *loved*. But it wasn't good enough to stay here. I'm so hurt. This place is so perfect and I most definitely do not fit in. Because I'm like that toy too—worn out and worthless to a guy like him.

'Talia—'

'It mightn't have met your standards but it was given with love and—'

He bends down to the bag at his feet and turns back to face me, his hand outstretched.

I'm instantly silenced. I stare at his hand and slowly take

the rabbit from him. His ear and head have been stitched back on properly.

'I wouldn't have thrown out a clearly much-loved toy, Talia.' His breathing is jumpy. 'I assumed it was one of *your* childhood toys. I didn't realise it had come from Romy. And I'm sorry if repairing it was the wrong thing to do.'

For a moment I struggle for air. Tears spring to my eyes as I study the soft little animal. I'm relieved. I'm touched. And I'm utterly embarrassed.

Swallowing hard, I run my finger over the neat stitching. 'You did this?'

'Yeah.'

'When?' I finally glance up at him.

He looks a little embarrassed. 'Before we drove to Dunedin.'

'You said you had work to do.' I try to smile but it doesn't really work. 'Did you lie to me?'

'This *was* work.' His shoulders lift. 'Of the unpaid parental kind.'

My heart absolutely melts.

'I didn't know toy surgery was on your CV.' But then he has a bunch of skills and talents.

'I'm sorry if I overstepped,' he says quietly.

'You didn't. You were really thoughtful.' Guilt washes over me. 'I just haven't had the time…'

'Because you've been doing those important things like keeping him alive.'

I shake my head as a tear runs down my cheek even though everything's okay now. Better than okay, in fact. 'I'm hormonal,' I mutter by way of an excuse as I brush it away.

He regards me with a smile that's both sweet and sceptical. 'I don't think it's hormones. I think you're tired and upset. Which isn't surprising, given how much you've had to process recently.'

But it's more than that. I've just blown up at him and he deserves to know why. Yet again he's shown me he can be trusted so he deserves to know that it isn't *him*.

'I don't have any toys from my childhood.' I rub the toy to soothe myself as I speak. 'I don't have anything at all, actually. So I want Lukas to have the toys he's been given.'

He cocks his head ever so slightly and it's just enough to tempt me to keep talking.

'You already know we moved a lot,' I mutter. 'I've lived in every city, most small towns in the country. Mum would pick us up from school and we'd just leave. She'd have broken up with the latest, or been abused by the guy's wife.' I wince, remembering how the daughter of one guy once shredded me at school. 'Mum would've packed a few clothes for us but never anything else—never any toys or anything. None of those little silly things I collected as a child. Things that shouldn't matter.'

'But do.'

I nod. 'So then you just accept it. That you're not going to keep them. So I stopped collecting.'

He's still as he listens.

'What little I have now I've got for myself, and even now I tend not to hold onto them any more. If you have less, then you don't feel a loss.' I shrug. 'Because if you haven't had something to begin with you can't really miss it...' I have no idea if I'm making sense to him but it's easier for me this way. It's emotional safety. 'Things don't last anyway, you know? Nothing is for ever.' But I run my fingers over the toy he's restored. He's fixed it so it *can* last longer.

'Right.' He slowly nods. 'But you want different for Lukas.'

I stare hard at the rabbit. 'Yep.'

'I get it.' He takes a step towards me. 'Both of us have parents who disappointed us.' He sighs and his smile is a little twisted. 'I had so *many* toys. Didn't love any of them.' He shoots me a rueful look. 'Poor little rich boy, right?' He bows his head. 'My parents behaved badly—either spoiling me or neglecting me, purely to antagonise each other. So I'm not unscathed. I have scars and triggers. Like I react badly when I think someone thinks the worst of my intentions. I still feel the shame and humiliation of having any private business aired. Their infidelities were exposed and picked over by everyone—gossiped about. They used me—taking me from school to go to a sports game but tipping off the press, one upping the other in spoiling me. But only in public—it was evidence-gathering for the lawyers and if there were no points to be gained the outing was abandoned.'

That he tells me this steals my breath. 'I'm sorry, Dain.'

He glances away, breaking that searing contact. I glance around too and it finally dawns on me that we're in his bedroom.

It's every bit as beautiful as the rest of the house—everything is gorgeous, it's jaw-dropping quiet luxury. But he's so used to it he doesn't seem to have any idea of how sumptuous everything in his life is. And I mean everything—from the private jet and gleaming cars to the discreet staff who appear and do things without him needing to direct them at all before melting into the shadows, to this palatial, magnificent home with every last detail and smallest fixture the absolute finest. Maybe his apparent unawareness is what happens when you're born into a family that's been wealthy for generations.

He could've gone out and bought a million new soft toys for Lukas. But he didn't—despite being surrounded by all this perfection. Because for all that wealth he was poor in other ways. He fixed up this old rabbit because he sensed its sentimental value.

'I'm still not sure he really fits in here even with the repair,' I mutter.

That Dain even knows how to stitch it stuns me. Surely he never had to darn his holey socks or anything. He'd have been handed new ones.

'He belongs with Lukas,' Dain says gruffly.

I glance back up at him only to see he's watching me and his expression isn't masked. I see his hunger. I see it and feel it and match it. I move closer.

He swallows but doesn't step back. He's watching me the way a predator watches the thing it wants. Warily, quietly, intensely—waiting for it to wander within reach.

I get that he doesn't trust people because they always have an ulterior motive. People want things—generally money—from him all the time. I don't want any of these *things* from him. At all. What I want is far more basic than that. Far more reckless. And it is so impossible to resist. But I should. For Lukas I should. For myself.

But the blue of Dain's eyes vanishes in the black heat of his pupils and the yearning I see echoes my own.

'Talia...'

I don't want him to think I want him because he's been nice—because he's helped me in so many ways already. It's frustrating and somehow I need to make that clear to him. 'I understand why you're not interested in marriage,' I say.

He stiffens. 'I've never wanted any kind of wife, trophy or otherwise. I can't commit to something I can't believe in.'

'Good.' I step towards him. 'Because *we're* definitely *not* getting married.'

He seems to stop breathing.

'Never, okay?' I whisper.

He tenses even more. I know he's reserved but he's very clear about what he *doesn't* want. I wouldn't consider this if I thought he had other intentions but there's honesty between us now. There's also this chemistry—it burns ever more intensely, ever more out of my control. I ache for touch. I stroke the toy I'm still holding instead. The toy he's fixed. Another wave of emotion engulfs me. I've misjudged him. Again.

'Never,' he finally agrees huskily. 'There's no reason for us to do something we know would be damaging to Lukas and to ourselves. We just…co-parent. Quietly and easily.' He stands very still. 'Lukas needs you. And you need…less stress.'

'I thought you said I needed to be indulged,' I say softly.

The words escape before my brain catches up—control slipping free of my hold, like water sinking through sand. But it's not a trickle, it's an unstoppable tsunami. I freeze but at the same time I really don't. I sway ever so slightly towards him. My body doesn't give a damn about the future. It's only interested in *now*.

'Talia…' he mutters a whispered warning.

I'm too far gone to pay heed. This passion between us is temporary. Such things are *always* temporary, right? This I know. All those men in my mother's life…

But I also know that *Dain* is not a cheater—I was wrong about that. He's reserved and private and wants to do his best for Lukas. He's gorgeous. And I can't resist this need any more. Because Dain will *always* do his best for Lukas—as will I. So I know he'll still work with me as best he can even after this chemistry fades. Neither of us wants Lukas to be caught up in arguing parents.

'So you want me to indulge you?' he says.

I lightly toss the toy to a side table so my hands are free. 'You wanted honesty, right?' I swallow. 'I still want you.' I touch his chest. 'I can't seem to stop wanting you.'

His hands span my waist and now I couldn't step back even if I wanted to.

I really don't want to. 'I don't want to complicate things but—'

'You can't get past it?' he interrupts with a growl.

'Right.' I nod. I can't *think*.

'Funny thing, nor can I.'

I'm so relieved my knees almost sag. 'We let it run…' I eventually say. 'Let it end.'

'And then move forward?' He's still but his hold on me tightens. 'For Lukas.'

'Yes.' I nod. 'We'll work it out for him. He'll always come first.'

'Right.' He leans towards me.

I truly do freeze now as his mouth drops towards mine. I shiver as he kisses me. And then I combust.

Throwing my arms around his neck, I kiss him back. He growls and moves swiftly, picking me up in his strong arms, dropping me onto his bed and tumbling on top. I moan in sheer relief. We're finally back on that page—the one we belong on together.

His hands sweep over me, swiftly stripping me. But suddenly he stops, a sharp drawn breath whistles between his teeth. I freeze and suddenly realise he's seen the red scar slicing across my lower abdomen. In the heat I've forgotten that I haven't told him.

'I had a C-section,' I whisper in hurried explanation. 'He was round the wrong way.'

My attempt to minimise it doesn't work. He rises above

me to look me in the eyes and the expression in his eyes makes me squirm with guilt.

'Were you scared?' He stares right through my defences.

'The doctors were great,' I mutter.

'Were you scared?' He tightens his grip on my wrists and leans closer over me. 'You didn't have a friend with you. No family.'

'I was okay,' I say. 'Most importantly Lukas was okay.'

I see the anger in his eyes. The hurt. I know he wants to rail at me. I see the ripple of emotion run through his body and his muscles bunch. I'm totally at his mercy and I deserve his wrath. But after the growl of annoyance from the back of his throat I feel an intimate caress so tender I quake. That's when I realise the punishment he intends for me to take is that of unbearable pleasure.

His exploration is slow and torturous. He kisses my scar reverently and then continues his exploration south, worshipping my body.

'I hate that you were alone,' he says huskily. 'All this time.'

I don't want him to be this gentle. This tender. I feel as if I don't deserve it. I shiver and try to pull back. But he grabs my hips and holds me still.

'I'm indulging you, Talia,' he whispers fiercely. 'You definitely should be indulged.'

'Even though I didn't tell you everything?'

'I've forgiven you.' He sighs roughly. 'Maybe it's time you forgive yourself on that.' He sits up and takes off his tee shirt in a wide, whipping movement.

I stare at him—made emotional by his words and overwhelmed by the sight of his body. Yep, I slither deeper into lust with him. That should be impossible. It should. I never realised I could want him more. But I do.

Neither of us were completely naked in the gondola. I've never actually been naked in front of a man before. But I'm not shy—he's always made this easy for me. And he's *stunning*. His lips curve as he sees me staring.

'I forgot,' he mutters. 'You like to look. You didn't really get the chance last time.'

He slowly strips the rest of his clothes for me. I'm so blown away by him all I can do is lie on his bed and stare.

He comes back to lean over me. 'You know you can touch if you want.'

I lift my hands and run them over his body but that's all I can do because he's back between my legs—teasing me so I'm only able to arch my hips closer and it's so erotic and so intimate I gasp.

'Let me indulge you,' he murmurs. 'Surrender to me, Talia.'

The sensations are so intense. I moan. Loudly.

He suddenly lifts away, rising up to kiss my mouth. Thoroughly. I stare at him questioningly when he lifts away to look into my eyes.

'Can't wake Lukas,' he murmurs in explanation. 'Don't want this interrupted before we've hardly begun.'

I've forgotten our son is sleeping in the room just down the hall—how terrible of me. He reads my mind and laughs again.

'You're allowed a little time for yourself,' he says. 'And you're definitely allowed a lot of time for *me*.'

That mix of arrogance and confident sensuality melts me. He moves back down my body and laughs again when he tastes for himself the effect his words have had on me.

'You're so deliciously responsive, Talia.'

That just makes me respond even more. I melt with his approval. And he works more than his tongue. He lets his fingers talk too. I gasp and bite down into the soft pillow to muffle my sighs and it's seconds, mere seconds, before I come hard.

I'm breathless but I know what I want—what I need—now. 'Dain.'

He glances up at me, a picture of hedonism sprawled between my legs. But as he sees my expression he frowns. 'Are you sure you're ready? It's not too soon?'

'It's not soon enough,' I mutter desperately. *'Please.'*

He flashes a tense smile at me. 'Okay.'

He leaves me for a moment and shoots me a rueful glance as he gets protection but, honestly, I'm too busy enjoying watching him get ready for me.

'I've also got protection of my own now,' I whisper, not wanting to hold anything back from him now. 'I talked it over with my doctors after Lukas's birth and they thought it might help regulate my cycle.' Which would make managing one thing a little easier.

'Two forms of protection is good,' he says gruffly.

'I think so too.' I smile at him.

He returns to the bed. I bite my lip—excited and a little apprehensive. He's big and strong and I'm neither. But he pulls me into his arms, sweeping a hand down my back, moulding me into his hard heat. I moan. He rolls, pinning me beneath him, and coaxes my legs further apart.

'You want me?'

There's a rawness to his question that pulls an equally harsh, honest response from me.

'Yes!'

He thrusts. Hard. He's inside me again and I'm a rippling, shivering, incoherent mess. Because it's good. He's good. He's in me, with me, and we're both so stunned it's a second before either of us can exhale.

'It's been so long,' he groans.

And then he moves. All I can do is wrap my arms around him because all I want is to keep him right here with me. I'm so close to him and I love it. This.

'You're as hot as you were that night.' His expression wild as he rears up and presses harder into me. 'So hot.'

He thrusts into me again and again and it's exquisite. I arch and cling, pushing to meet him with every wild movement. It's the best thing ever and once again it's shockingly quick. I go as tense as a wire. Next second my body is so crunched in ecstasy that my soul-piercing scream is silent.

I keep my eyes closed, because as I struggle to catch my breath I realise an alarming truth.

I'm never going to get enough of this.

I'm never going to get enough of *him*.

CHAPTER SIXTEEN

Dain

I CANCEL BUSINESS trips and make video calls instead. Even then I've cleared my schedule more than I ever have. I don't want to leave them. Not for fear she'll walk out on me. She's slept in my bed every night since I brought her here. She can't get enough of me and I'm the same for her. I don't dwell on that fact too long. It'll ebb. These things always do.

So I'll just enjoy the fact we now have a nanny for night time. Even so I'm trying not to be too demanding so Talia can catch up on some of the sleep she's been short of for months. But actually, despite my best intentions, she thwarts me—she's demanding and playful. I relish the challenge of keeping up with her. Her unexplored passionate side has been fully revealed and it's a seemingly bottomless well of want.

I go to Lukas in the mornings. I love 'talking' with him first thing. I scoop him up and change him and bring him to Talia. His smiles have developed to laughter and babbling. I don't recognise my own spontaneity. Since when do I work from home? Since when do I delegate meetings? But I'm a father playing catch-up with his firstborn. I don't want to leave them for hours at a time and go to work. I've lost so much time I don't want to miss a moment more.

I know Talia feels as though she doesn't fit. I know she has a fear of loss. But I can protect her here in my home and there's one more thing I can do to cement her security. I work with the lawyers via video link then take the paperwork to her at lunch.

'What's this?' She's instantly wary, which makes me tense up totally.

'It's Lukas's reissued birth certificate,' I say. 'Your contract. Plus some other papers.'

'My contract? For what? I don't need a contract.'

I glare at her. 'Can you give me just five minutes before interrupting with your rejection?'

She shoots me a mulish look. 'I don't understand what you're doing. Or why this is even necessary.'

'So that no matter what happens to me, or what happens between us, you and Lukas will have a home. Always.'

'I thought we'd agreed on that already,' she says shortly. 'I trust you.'

My heart stalls. 'Right.' I clear my throat. 'This is just the documentation to prove it.' And then some, actually, but I'm a bit thrown.

'What about this?' She points to one of the papers.

'My life insurance policy. It'll be worth it for you if I die.'

Her flushed cheeks are leeched of colour in a second. 'You think I'd want Lukas to lose a parent?'

'Talia…' I feel terrible. I just hit her with casually cruel words. My parents were so good at it. Knowing where and how to strike to inflict maximum emotional damage. I'm screwing up already. I could hurt her. Hurt Lukas. I don't ever want to. In part that's why it's important to me to get this paperwork squared away. So that if—*when*—things go south between us, everything is still sorted for Lukas. And her.

'I'm sorry,' I mutter. 'That was insensitive.'

She looks troubled more than hurt. 'You realise he needs *you*, not your money.'

I stare at her.

'*You're* worth far more than any amount of money,' she adds as if I haven't grasped it already.

I feel awkwardness heat my face.

'And *I* don't want your money.'

Yeah, I've got that message, actually. She's already given back the money that I put in her account. I understand why she did it. If our positions were reversed I'd have done the same. Even so, it annoys me immensely.

'You never have to worry about not having a home. Or not having enough ever again. You never have to worry about this being taken away from you or having to just up and leave.'

Her face pales and I know I've hurt her by reminding her of the past, but the point is she's through that now. 'You know it's nothing to me.' And there are no conditions.

'It's not nothing. You can't do things like this for everyone or you won't be a billionaire for very much longer.'

'You're not everyone,' I mutter through gritted teeth. 'You're the *mother* of my *child*.'

She stiffens, and somehow I feel as if I've said the wrong thing.

'I don't want a massive disparity between his parents' lives,' I try to explain, but I'm making it worse. 'I don't want him subjected to bitter comparisons—'

'You mean when we live separately.'

I hesitate. We haven't talked about the future and it feels like boggy ground to cover now. I don't want to go there.

I don't want to think on it. Not yet. We're still letting that chemistry run. 'You let me give Ava money.'

'Yes, and that benefitted me. *That* was enough,' she says passionately. 'This, for *Lukas*, I understand. That you want to make his future secure no matter what. But this isn't what *I* want from you.'

There's suddenly an undercurrent between us that I'm wary of exploring.

What does she want? What does she really want from me?

I don't want to know. It's safer to retreat.

'If you don't want to touch the money, then don't,' I grit. 'Earn your own and save my unwanted amount for Lukas.'

'I will,' she says firmly. 'I'll do exactly that.'

'Great.'

She turns away from me. I'm not sure if I've angered or pleased her. I shake my head as I walk away. I really need to get to the office and get myself back on track.

I last less than three hours at the office. It's too soon to be there, right? I need to make sure they're okay. Talia's not in the main house and for a moment panic flares before my groundsman quietly tells me she's at the pool house.

There I stop in the doorway, stunned at the scene. Those boxes are open but things are *not* organised. There are beans and froth and coffee grounds everywhere. A million lattes are scattered over the bench, each with intricate designs on the top. There's music quietly playing and randomly she's in a bikini. The whole thing makes me smile. My heart sings. My body has its usual reaction—on steroids. But as much as I ache for her right now I don't want to interrupt her and take her from her happy place. I step back but she catches sight of me.

'Hey.' Her smile is huge.

It's all the invitation I need. I step forward, warmth flowing through me already. 'What are you doing?' Duh. As if it isn't obvious.

'Making use of Lukas's nap time,' she says. 'We had a swim earlier hence...' She glances down at the bikini she's wearing. 'I got this from that drawerful in the wet room. They're all new. All sizes catered to.' She pauses. 'For your guests?'

I shrug but the possessive thread in her question makes me even hotter. 'Did Lukas enjoy the water?'

'Loved it until he got completely over-tired. The nanny took him inside.'

I wish I'd been here to play in the pool with them both. 'And you decided to do some content creation. In your bikini.'

'Of course,' she answers, with a nonchalance that's undermined by her sparkling gaze. 'You said this was my kitchen to do whatever I wanted in.'

'You're saying you're the boss in here?'

'Yes.' She caresses me, tugging at my suit. 'You're a little overdressed for such a warm day.'

Oh, another invitation I cannot resist. 'You think? What would you advise me to do?'

Her smile is positively wicked. 'I think you should strip.'

I laugh at the eagerness in her expression. 'You want me to dance for you.'

The tip of her tongue touches her lip. 'Would you?'

Her playfulness delights me. This is Talia at her best—confident and relaxed, doing what she loves and teasing me too boot. So of course—despite my inner awkwardness—I begin. But the way she watches, the way she breathes—any last inhibition vanishes. I'm confident in my body but this is next level. This is about seeing her glaze over.

Her hands are at my waist. Firm hands. She pushes and I let her spin me so I'm the one with my back to the kitchen counter. She steps forward and pushes me another pace so the wood is flush against my butt. She takes my hands and spreads my arms, placing my palms down on the counter behind me.

She's fast. And she's breathless. It's an effort for her to unzip my trousers. I grip the counter to stop myself taking hold of her. Taking over. That she's initiated this makes me harder than ever. Like that night in the gondola, when she was shy but forward, curious as hell. I ache to hear her little laugh again but I'm helpless to do anything now—I'm utterly in thrall to her next movement.

'What do you think you're doing?' I gasp.

'What do you think I'm doing?'

'Control freak,' I mutter. 'Always needing to be in charge.'

'And there's you, always needing to know every last little thing.'

Our lips brush but she pulls away playfully quick. Her breasts almost touch my chest. Desire whispers between us, a dangerous thread that's about to ignite.

She works down my chest. Licks my abs. Lust clouds her eyes as she takes me in hand and I get how much she wants this. I'm so damn grateful because I want it too. More than anything. I lose everything in this heat between us. I forget the impossible issues. The old anger that underlies my very existence. There's just this. I shake with sheer delight in a single stroke of her tongue and the playful scrape of her teeth devastates me. And when I see her eyes I really start to lose it. She's got this dreamy look and her cheeks are flushed and I realise she's loving doing this to me as much as I love being on the end of her dangerously provocative mouth. I want to stroke her. To make her come with me. I don't want to be alone in this—

'Dain...' she sighs. It's the sound of desire.

Yeah, I'm not alone. I gasp as I realise how aroused she is. I thread my fingers through her hair and she takes me deep into the back of her throat. I can't hold back. Her hand tightens and her mouth—her hot, wet mouth—pulls. I babble her name over and over, begging her to finish me—

It tears through me in a white-hot convulsion. She holds me through it, taking everything I release into her, until I sag back against the counter. Reduced to nothing. Barely able to stand. I blink hazily and watch my vixen rise to her feet in front of me. I'm all but catatonic as she licks her lips. Her eyes now sparkle and her cheeks are flushed. And then she laughs.

The resurgence of energy is instant and stunning. I was wiped out only moments ago but now I want to reduce her to the same incoherent, slick mess of arousal that she made me. I touch her with as much tenderness as I can muster and discover she's already there.

'Oh, you enjoyed me,' I growl with voracious delight.

Her eyes glaze. 'Yes.'

Sex usually brings me emotional oblivion. But this isn't oblivion. I'm *here* with her—more present than I've ever been in my life. I want to see her. Taste her. Please her to the point where she can't speak any more. Where she can't deny me anything.

'My turn,' I rumble.

She yelps as I lift her onto the counter. And then she laughs. She lets me have her body. In this realm she grants me permission for everything.

And I take it.

CHAPTER SEVENTEEN

Talia

HE SLIDES HIS palm up to hold me by the side of my neck, tilting my head back so my mouth is in place to meet his.

'You realise it's my turn to be in charge.' His eyes glitter.

He's hoarse and he's flushed and his muscles jump beneath my fingertips. He pulls my hands off him and presses them to my breasts.

'Play with yourself while I feast.'

My jaw drops. He grunts a laugh and kisses me. His hands cover mine, pushing my fingers to pinch my tight nipples. I'm already hot from having him at my mercy only minutes ago. From feeling him pump into my mouth. But now I'm his plaything and I obey.

'Good girl.'

I gasp as that edge of arousal sharpens.

He tugs my bikini bottoms. I quickly wriggle to help him. I'm so eager I ought to be embarrassed but he just praises me again and I liquefy on the counter before him. He drags his hot open mouth down my body—from plundering my mouth, to suck my neck and down my sternum— a direct line down my centre until he hits that sensitive part of me. He's not merciful. He's avaricious. He wants all of me—my absolute surrender. He laughs as I writhe, desperate for the release he withholds from me. His fingers flicker and invade, filling the aching void inside me while his tongue teases—rewarding me.

The convulsions overwhelm me almost instantly—wave after wave of an exquisitely intense orgasm that goes on for a mind-blowingly long time. I try to slow my breath. It doesn't work.

'You don't think you're done, do you?' He teases a finger up the inside of my thigh.

My mouth feels tender but I manage to smile at him. He sweeps my mussed-up hair from my face and smiles back. He's the sexiest thing I've ever seen.

He's hard again and just like that I'm ready again too. He pulls me so I'm on the edge of the counter and presses close. I cry out with guttural completion as he fills me. His powerful thrusts almost shunt me away from him. He grunts and tightens his arm around my waist to hold me closer and closer as he rams more deeply inside me. I curl my legs around his hips to help—to lock him to me. It's hot and fast and we're both slick so we clutch each other even harder and it's like nothing ever. I'm barely on the counter, he's taking almost all my weight and its so, *so* good that in the end all I can do is scream in supreme satisfaction.

It takes an age for me to blink my way back to reality. I turn my head to rest it on his sweat-slicked shoulder and that's when I see the tripod. And the little red light. Flashing.

'Oh!' I gasp. 'Oh, *no*!'

'What's wrong?' He eases away enough to look into my face.

I push him further so there's enough space that I can slip down from the counter. 'I'm still filming,' I mutter.

'What?' His eyes widen. 'You're what?'

'The cameras. They're on.'

He freezes. 'Not live streaming?'

Panic washes over me as I double-check. 'No.' Relief is instant. 'No.' I stop the recording and release a shaky breath. 'Just recording.'

But that's bad enough. I flush from the top of my scalp to the tips of my toes. The things these cameras have just seen? Dain will be horrified.

But his mouth twitches as he watches me press my hands to my hot forehead. 'Have we inadvertently made our own movie?' He cocks his head. 'You should see your face right now...'

Yep, I bet. I'm an enormous beetroot.

Both cameras were filming as I worked on my latte art and then I saw him and just got distracted and all that time when we were on the bench doing...very adult things... there was a camera filming. Two cameras, in fact.

He catches my eye and to my amazement that twitch at the corner of his mouth becomes a full-blown grin and next minute we're both helplessly giggling like absolute fools to the point where I have to wipe tears from my eyes.

I guess it's the endorphin release—the lingering pleasure of those moments, followed by total panic and then sheer relief that the world hasn't just been privy to them.

Dain disappears into the other room and reappears in a robe, holding another that he wraps me in.

'We have to delete them...' I mutter apologetically as he fastens the waist belt of my robe for me. But I'm engulfed by a wave of heat as I recall just what's been captured on film. 'We should do that right away,' I add, stupidly flustered.

'Sure,' he says easily, but there's a devilish glint in his

eyes as he studies my face up close. 'If that's what you want…'

'It is. Absolutely. That footage can't survive,' I immediately respond and then look at him. 'Don't you think?'

Of course he does. He's all about privacy and having as little online as possible. This would be a nightmare for him, right?

But he just raises an eyebrow at me. 'Don't you think we should watch it first?'

I gape at him and suddenly I'm awash with a hot flush even worse than before.

But he's flushed too, and he crowds me even though he's wrapped me in the soft silk robe already. 'You can see for yourself how beautiful you are when you lose total control.'

Oh. My.

'Dain…' I'm so flustered I can hardly say his name.

He chuckles. 'You don't think it would be fun?'

My heart races. Curiosity has me. As does the amusement in his eyes. He can be ridiculously fun. He reads my expression and his own lights up.

'I'll get the popcorn.' He turns to the nearest cupboard.

He makes me giggle again. I feel reckless and wanton and naughty and it is so liberating. He grabs the cameras in one hand and takes my hand in the other and leads me into the large comfortable lounge that overlooks that deep blue pool.

I had no idea who Dain Anzelotti was, that night in the gondola. The lifestyle he lives is so foreign to anything I've ever experienced. Things that he doesn't even notice take my breath away. The private jet. The people quietly attending to his every need. The fine silk perfectly tailored to skim a body sustained by meals whipped up by an award-winning private chef. But none of that is relevant right now. It's just him and me—teasing each other, being free with each other.

It's only because of one passionate whim, a wisp of recklessness in one moment, that we're together again. I know these are a fantasy few days and they're not for ever.

He splits the enormous smart screen hanging on the wall so the footage from both cameras plays simultaneously side by side. There's a bird's-eye angle from above us and a side-profile angle. He fiddles so we get the sound from only one of the cameras and it plays low on the speaker. There is music playing but I can still hear our conversation.

Dain takes a seat right behind me on the rug—encircling me. Neither of us eat the popcorn. I stare at the screen— riveted—half appalled. In the next moment I'm fully aroused. It was steamy at the time, now it's just smoking hot and I'm toast.

There's his dance. There's me dropping to my knees and—

This time I can see his face, not just feel his reaction. I can see the size of him, the strain of his body—arching towards my touch. The way he looks at me as I pleasure him turns me to goo. I can't sit still as I watch him then lift and spread me on that counter. Hearing his words—what he's going to do to me—then seeing him do it to me is as hot as the moment it actually happened. Which honestly ought to be impossible.

'What do you think?' His breath stirs my hair.

I can't look away from the screen but from behind he loosens my robe and touches me. He begins with my breasts but then one hand glides lower. I moan as I realise how wet I am in this instant but he tells me how good it is. How good I am. That he's turned on too and he can't wait to taste me again. And then I'm wetter still. And that just makes him double his words of approval because it means I'm ready to take him again and he really needs me to be ready—

'See?' He nips the side of my neck tenderly as he lifts me onto his lap and gives me everything I want in a slow, searing slide. 'You're so beautiful when you let me indulge you.'

I quiver in a mini release right away, because he's so big and so hard and it's just what I want. He groans as I take him to the hilt.

The action on the screen is fast and energetic, but his possession of me now is lush and lazy and total. He teases me intimately, so lightly with the tips of his fingers, so I grind on him harder, clenching within to lock him inside. He swears in earthy, guttural delight. I'm just utterly incoherent. Again. I don't watch the climax on screen, I'm too busy having another.

It's quite some time before I can speak again. He's stretched out on the rug and taken me down with him and is holding me close. I've never experienced physical intimacy or pleasure like this. He's playful and inventive and every time I'm left a shaking mess. It doesn't get easier. It doesn't lessen in intensity. It's always unbearably exciting. And I can't get enough.

As if he knows how raw I feel he caresses my back with long, light, tender strokes that slowly soothe my oversensitive soul. 'Still want to delete it?'

I lift my head just enough to see his face. He's flushed and handsome and like a pirate.

'I...'

Can't think when he smiles at me like that.

His smile is the most powerful weapon I've ever encountered. All I can do is smile back. 'I can't believe we did any of that.'

'Yeah.' He strokes my cheek. 'Shall we go back to the house—?'

'And see Lukas.' I finish his thought.

He smiles even more. Then he unplugs the cameras from the screen and puts them in my hand. He curls my trembling fingers around them so I don't drop them because I'm still so weak I'm butterfingered. 'You should keep the recording to remember. Or replay again some time. It's yours. Always. You decide what to do with it,' he says. 'I trust you.'

I can't believe he's given me this thing that is unbelievably personal. This is a man who loathes anything private being played out in public. A man who does the almost impossible to ensure any digital trace of him is erased. A man who values nothing more than his privacy.

'I could sell this for money, Dain Anzelotti…' I mutter. 'I could put this online.'

'You could. But I know you won't.' He smiles slightly. 'Your reputation, remember? You once said your career would be ruined by an association with me.'

'While you said it would be enhanced.' But I smile at him shyly. 'You trust me with this.'

I'm touched. His trust is a gift more precious than any *thing*.

I don't want to delete it. Ever. I don't want to lose anything from these days because I know this isn't going to last. But I realise this film isn't ever going to be enough. I want and need the real thing—*him*—again and again and again.

CHAPTER EIGHTEEN

Dain

I ADORE TEASING HER. It's so easy. She's so responsive. So satisfying. I race home early every day—well, the days I actually make it to work in the first place. Almost a week has passed in a fog of lusty laughter—it's light and crazy easy.

But it can't last much longer. The whispers have begun. It was inevitable—the leak wouldn't have been one of my staff but perhaps a delivery driver, or maybe someone saw us at the airport. Who knows? But I've had more calls to my private number in the last week than I've had in months and I can't continue to ignore their questions. While I try to maintain a low public profile, people pay attention. I'm worth a lot of money, plus I'm in charge of a lot of other people's fortunes. I have thousands of contractors counting on me plus high-paying customers, and we'll keep those customers only if the reputation of my company remains pristine. And I am my company. It's my name on the door. If my personal life becomes the story, then the company suffers. That's what happened with my parents and I won't let it happen again.

So I need to show my face at headquarters, do some site visits and restore balance—the pendulum has swing too far. I also need to own my new personal situation. The only way is to front-foot it.

I'll never bow to the external pressure to do that traditional 'right thing', the sexist instruction to 'make an honest woman of her'—it's old-fashioned and unnecessary. And it doesn't work. We won't make our parents' mistakes. We'll see this through then care for Lukas like the responsible adults we are.

I find her in the pool house and, confronted with her beauty, I can't resist kissing her so it's a few moments before I can speak.

'Unfortunately, despite my best efforts at total privacy, the rumour mill is rumbling.' I sigh. 'You need to meet my parents. We need to introduce Lukas to them first.'

'Your *parents*?' She pulls back, stunned. 'You're still in contact with them?'

Yeah, if I had more of a choice I wouldn't be. 'They're shareholders.'

Her jaw drops.

'*Minority* shareholders,' I clarify. 'Part of the divorce settlement and my buy-out when I took over.' I reduced their impact but couldn't cut them out completely and they still talk. So even though I rarely see them I know I need to include them in this. But in my own way. 'Confidence in the company—therefore in me—is essential. Curiosity has been roused. I need to take control of the narrative.'

'Of course you do.' She rolls her eyes.

I laugh as I tug her closer. 'Don't worry. They're too wrapped up in their own war to give a damn about you.'

'They're still fighting?'

She has no idea.

'They'll go to their graves fighting. The bitterness is next level.'

'I thought they divorced when you were—'

'Fourteen, yeah.'

'That's a while ago.' She draws in a deep breath. 'How will you introduce me? Am I a friend, casual acquaintance, captive?'

Oh, she makes me smile. 'We don't need to define anything. They can think whatever they want.'

'And how's that controlling the narrative?'

She's right but I don't like considering these details too closely. The complications my fractured family could bring stress me out. 'We'll fake it.' I snap decide. 'No reason they won't believe us. Like we did with Ava. You've only just agreed to come back with me. I've had to work at it. You took some convincing.'

'No one's going to believe that.'

'You don't think you exude cool indifference? That you're not an impervious, powerful woman?'

'Cool indifference?' She looks sceptical.

'Yeah. Infinitely capable and needing no one.'

'That's not possible. Everyone needs someone sometimes.'

I'm distracted by her. 'Do you ever need someone?'

She angles her head. 'Sometimes in a dark, dangerous, life-threatening moment I don't want to be alone.'

Her mouth mocks but her eyes flicker and I know she actually means it.

'You want someone's hand to hold?' I ask quietly.

She stares intently at me and her smile slowly softens. 'Brief me on how you want me to handle them.'

I feel a wave of gratitude for her attempt to make this easy for me and suddenly I don't hold back on the truth. 'They're coming tomorrow night.'

'Tomorrow?' Her eyes widen. 'Decisive.'

'Best-case scenario it'll be a stilted and uncomfortable Cold War situation. My mother will ask me directly for money. My father will have a business idea he wants to run past me after dinner. A quick pull aside. It won't be quick. They'll both be disappointed. They'll each blame me for being too much like the other. It'll devolve into an argument between them.'

Honestly, it'll be a timely reminder of everything I don't want.

'You don't want to invite them individually?' she asks.

'And have one outraged because they weren't the one to meet Lukas *first*?'

'That would happen?'

'Absolutely.'

She looks wary now. 'Do you want them to be a big presence in Lukas's life?'

'I need to show respect and let them know he exists, but he won't become a pawn between them. Ever.'

She nods but her tension doesn't lessen. 'Will they disapprove of me?'

My skin tightens. She's vulnerable. 'One will, one won't. Purely to disagree with each other so it doesn't actually matter what you do or say, they'll just take a side as soon as one stakes a claim either way. Don't worry about it and for heaven's sake don't take it personally.' But of course there's no way she won't take it personally. I'm hit with a tardy premonition that this is a bad idea. 'You know, maybe you don't have to be there…'

Now she looks even more tense.

'I don't want to stress you out,' I explain quickly. '*I* find it stressful enough.'

But to my surprise the pinched look slowly leaves her

face and she lifts her chin. 'They're your parents, naturally
it's more stressful for you.'

'I'm used to it.' I shrug.

'Well, now you don't have to face them alone.' She flicks
her hair back like a diva. 'I've dealt with the rudest, most
obnoxious customers. Your parents will be a cinch.'

It was worse than I'd predicted. *Stupid.* I don't want to discuss it. Don't want to meet her eyes. Can't believe I let her
see it. *So stupid.*

She's silent and the staff have taken away the barely
touched dinner plates. We're standing on the veranda in
darkness, having watched my parents drive off in their
separate cars.

'Can you not…feel sorry for me?' I mutter.

'You don't want me to feel for you?'

Something inside me twists. I'm lost for words.

'They treat you terribly,' she says. 'It's shocking.'

Her saying it aloud makes it worse. I regret inviting my
parents here more than ever. Not because I can't handle seeing them, but I can't handle Talia seeing the truth. 'Don't—'

'I'm sorry you went through all that with them.' She ig-
nores my quiet plea. 'At least I had Ava, but you were alone.'

'Not completely,' I murmur. 'I had my grandfather for
a while.'

'Lukas senior.' She leans against the veranda railing and
gazes across the gardens even though it's too dark to see
much. 'You looked close in that photo.'

The one photo I allowed to remain on the company website. 'Right.'

I thought we were.

Silence again. I chance a glance at her. In the moon-
light she's so pretty. I've mostly seen her with her hair tied

up—a messy top knot or a high ponytail—but tonight she let her hair loose. It's long and glossy and now I can't take my gaze off her. I ache to snake my arm around her waist and feel that contact with her. I want it to be like the gondola when the rest of the world disappeared and there was only the two of us.

Her expression softens as she looks back at me. She doesn't say anything. She doesn't pry any further and I appreciate that restraint.

'I was sent to boarding school in my early teens. I appreciated it, to be honest. It got me away from the week about war with Mum and Dad. They were in separate houses by then and fighting over everything, including me. But neither really wanted me, I was just a useful weapon. Weekends and holidays were still a battleground, same with school events. They'd argue over who got to attend the sports day and then either they'd both show and cause a scene or neither would show up. That's when my grandfather stepped in.' I found solace with him for a time.

I don't know why I'm telling her when I can't stand the sympathy I already see in her eyes. But I can't stop myself babbling on because seeing my parents tonight brought it all back up. And being with Lukas and knowing I never, ever want him to feel anything like I did. Talia needs to understand why that is so we can be sure to work through this together. That's why she needs to know, right? For Lukas.

'He was my escape from them. I'd go there for every holiday and every other chance I could. I adored him and we bonded over the business. He taught me a lot about it—the history, his dreams for it. I knew it was tearing him apart to see my parents neglect it because they were too busy fighting each other. It became both our hope for me to turn it around in the future.'

'And you did.'

'Eventually, yeah.' After he died.

She nods and we're silent for a while.

'I wasn't told he had terminal cancer,' I mumble quietly.

She jerks and looks at me again.

Even though I now know the reasons why, it still hurts. 'It was weird at first. He stopped replying to my messages, didn't take my calls. I got through to his secretary and was told he was too tired to see me. It was so sudden I didn't know what I'd done wrong. But it had to be something.' My chest tightens. 'I wasn't to come home to his house from school. I was to stay and study because he was busy now and didn't have time to see me.'

'Are you saying your grandfather ghosted you?'

'Basically. Yeah.' I roll my shoulders, unable to ease the tension building inside. 'I didn't study though. I spent the semester wondering what I'd done to make him stop—'

I break off. I don't use the 'L' word. But that was how it felt—that he'd stopped loving me. He'd stopped letting me be in his life. Because I'd done something bad and I didn't know what.

'It was Simone who told me in the end. The media were about to break the story that Lukas, the Anzelotti patriarch, was terminal and there was going to be all-out war between my parents for the company majority. It was salacious and cruel. Simone came to the boarding school and smuggled me out, furious that I hadn't been given any warning.'

'Did you get to him?'

'My parents met me. It was the one time I saw them united. They said the truth had been kept from me to protect me. They didn't want me to be distracted from my schoolwork. They wanted me to do well in my exams.' My fingers tighten on the railing. 'This supposed concern from the people who'd been distracting me for *years* with their bitter fights.'

'That must have been really—'

'Shit? Yeah, it was. Because they'd done it at my grandfather's insistence. He'd said he would change his will if they didn't both toe the line on it.' I glance at her and can't get my voice above a whisper. 'It was *his* call.'

'Did you get to spend time with him before he died?'

'No.'

'Dain, that's… I'm so sorry.' Her eyes are bright. 'So when you found I'd kept Lukas from you—'

'Yeah, low moment.' I don't want to go there again. We're past it. I half regret saying anything at all.

'And you were angry about my not having told Ava,' she says.

'I felt for her.' I clench my gut. 'I know what it's like to be kept in the dark. It makes you feel…incompetent.' Rejected.

'No wonder you keep people at a distance.'

Her expression eases the ache in my chest but at the same time causes another to build. I ache to hold her. I ache for the balm of her soft body resting against mine. I've never needed physical comfort like this before. Sex is only fun. It's only a moment—a great release—then I walk away. But this isn't that. I freeze because I don't understand it. I don't welcome it. I don't *want* this change. I don't want to *need* anyone the way I need her right now. I grip the railing to stop myself moving to her. Only it hurts to resist the urge.

'Dain…'

My throat aches. I can't answer her. But I can't send her away either. And I can't take my gaze from her.

Her smile is sad. 'You're so guarded.'

Maybe. Yeah. I've never told anyone about my grandfather's decision. It was far too painful to utter aloud. I probably shouldn't have done it now. I make myself turn away and bow my head. I wait for her to leave. Expect her to.

There's silence. But then I feel her hand slide onto mine.

'I don't blame you for that,' she breathes. 'It's okay.'

On auto I release the railing and turn my hand to lace my fingers through hers. I lock them together. Us together. She wraps her other arm around me, her palm pressing flat just below my ribs, her stomach flush against my back. For a long time we stand linked like that. I'm silent, sandwiched between the railing and her, and it's oddly, overwhelmingly safe.

Compassion. It's an altogether different feeling from any I've felt with her. No less powerful. If anything, it's…*more.* I can't remember the last time someone just hugged me like this and the warmth and weight of her leaning against me is so soothing I don't ever want to move.

'Sometimes families just suck,' she whispers.

I half laugh and that horrible tension, the agony, that's been twisting me up all night finally eases. 'Yeah.'

CHAPTER NINETEEN

Talia

I DON'T SLEEP WELL. Dain brings Lukas early in the morning for me to feed him, then takes him to change and dress. Now they're engrossed in one of their endless nonsensical conversations. Dain's chattier with his son than anyone and I can hardly bear to look at them. Lukas is the sweetest thing I've ever seen while Dain's the sexiest. My heart twists at the joy they've found in each other. I don't want anything to come between them or to damage the relationship now building between them. Especially not me.

I leave the room and go to shower, still processing what I witnessed last night. It was a revelation. I don't think I was any help—*sometimes families suck*—I wince at my tragic attempt at comfort. But it's true, right? And wouldn't it be good to pick your own? If I could choose, I'd keep both these guys so close.

But Dain doesn't want that and after last night I really understand why. Dinner with his parents was worse than he prepared me for. He diverted conversation. Distracted. Deflected. He worked so hard I was exhausted just watching him. They were sad, selfish people who complained and contradicted each other from the moment they arrived.

Over who got to hold Lukas first even—over everything. The constant point-scoring shocked me. Ultimately they just want things from Dain—money most especially. He's never been valued for himself. No wonder he doesn't trust anyone.

He was still charming to them, but I saw glimpses of a child desperate to please, to placate, to make everything better and bring peace to his world. I get it, I'm the same. I'm only capable and efficient because I had to be. But Ava loves me, and Romy supported me, and Dain himself has been wonderful to me. But he didn't have that. No wonder his relationship with his family is fractured. No wonder he fiercely guards his privacy. No wonder he fights hard to retain control over everything in his life.

I realise now that he has walls that I can't breach. And even though I know they're awful people, their judgement of me was obvious. It doesn't just hurt. It makes me nervous. I know he and I have some things in common— lust for each other especially—but not enough of the *right* things.

I don't know that I can exist in his world. If I were on the staff, sure—but as his supposed equal?

'Want to come on an adventure with me?' Dain asks the second I walk into the living room.

'An adventure? Where?' Just like that I'm diverted.

He smiles at my immediate interest. 'You and me, only for a couple of hours. Lukas will be better off here than where we're going.'

Of course I can't resist. I kiss Lukas and leave him with the nanny. Dain guides me to the garage on the edge of his property. I've not been in there yet, and in the doorway I stop and blink. There are several cars lined up neatly inside. All of them are very fancy.

'You have a collection?' I tease.

'Only a little one. Of only the best ones.' He flashes a smile. 'Don't hold it against me.'

I don't. I chuckle. We have a very different attitude to *things*—I don't collect, he does. But now it's only things he truly appreciates. And I can appreciate that quirk of his today because the sleek two-seater convertible sports car he selects has heated leather seats and it's sheer luxurious fun to cruise with the top down and feel the wind in my hair.

It's so early there's surprisingly little traffic and we arrive at a marina in no time. An astonishing array of boats gleams on the pristine blue water.

Butterflies flutter in my belly. 'How many are yours?' I cover it with a joke.

'Only the one.'

'The biggest?'

He laughs and then looks at me with gentle understanding. 'You okay at the thought of going on the water? It's a beautiful morning. Calm, pristine conditions.'

'You're saying I'm going to be safe.'

'I wouldn't risk you,' he says softly.

I know. Because of Lukas.

'You can hold my hand if you want.' He holds his palm towards me.

I take it.

We board a gleaming white catamaran. I feel as if I've stepped into a film set, only it's real. The crew are lined up to meet me. They're dressed immaculately and are so polite, so well drilled in their job he doesn't need to issue orders. Everything is beautiful and perfect, it's like magic. I know it's not just that they're paid a mint to do it. I get the feeling they *want* to do a good job for him—same with the discreet staff at his house. They're loyal because they actually like him.

He's *not* as entitled as I first thought. Yes, he was born into wealth, but he worked hard to turn the family company around when it foundered. He's worked hard to get what he has. And he's working hard to please me now.

'Aren't you going to captain the ship?' I ask once the crew disappear to get ready to move.

'Not this time,' he says lazily. 'I'm going to breakfast with you.'

'But you can, right? You have your boat licence and a whole other bunch of licences, right?'

'Right now I'm hoping for a licence to eat,' he teases.

I follow him up to the large back deck and see the feast already set there.

'When did you arrange this?' I ask.

He just smiles. I blink repeatedly at the beautiful view— and I don't mean the bay. I'm too blown away by him to nibble on the fresh fruit and pastries.

'Nothing tempts?' He notices. 'The chef will make you something fresh if you want?'

Laughing, I shake my head. 'I'm too busy taking in the view. The water looks so inviting—'

'You want to swim?' His eyebrows lift. 'It's not too cold?'

'This is warm for me.' I smile. Even though it's technically still winter, it's much hotter here in Brisbane than back in the South Island of New Zealand. 'But no, I don't want to swim.'

'But you want to strip?' He teases.

I just want to stare. At him. Which I don't. I make myself look beyond him. We glide over the blue waters passing beautiful bays with gleaming gold sand. It's invigorating and my heart soars.

'I've never been sailing,' I chirrup thoughtlessly, turning to look at him again. I never imagined *ever* being on a boat like this.

Again he just smiles. He knows. Of course he knows that there are lots of things I've never done. I bow my head to hide the burn of embarrassment—I'm so *gauche*. But he lifts my chin, forcing me to meet his intense blue gaze again.

'There's no shame in never having gone sailing before,' he says softly. 'But now you can. With me.' He pulls me close. 'We'll come back—scuba when it's warmer.'

'I don't know how to scuba.'

'I'll teach you.'

'You're a qualified scuba coach as well?'

He chuckles.

My heart thunders. 'Why did you arrange this?'

He waves a hand. 'It's a beautiful morning.'

'You don't have work to do?'

'Maybe we both deserve a little break from work. You've been working your whole life too.'

My lips twist. 'You've got bigger rewards, though.'

He gazes towards the bay. 'I don't mind sharing with you.'

For a moment I'm speechless.

'Thank you for helping me with Ava,' I eventually say. 'Thank you for this. Thank you for everything.'

His expression closes. 'You know I don't want your gratitude.'

'Too bad.' I shrug. 'You'll get used to it eventually.'

His mouth twists. 'And maybe you'll eventually get used to getting what you actually deserve.'

CHAPTER TWENTY

Dain

I WATCH THE flush cover her face. She doesn't feel it, does she? *Deserving*. Given her parents' abandonment and self-ishness, maybe that's not surprising. But she's spent years making her own way, caring for her sister without any help…she should feel *proud* of all that. Surely she's proved her worth to herself?

I really want her to have some fun and I've seen her in my pool throughout the week. It seems that, like me, she loves the water.

'What else can we add to the list?' I ask as I reach for a glass of fresh orange juice to ease the dryness of my throat. 'Stand-up paddle boarding in Croatia? Jet-skiing in Dubai?' I warm to my theme. 'Snorkelling in the Cay-mans? Water-skiing in—'

'I have been water-skiing,' she interrupts. 'Once.'

I'm instantly curious and lean close.

She reads my expression and laughs a little bitterly. 'It wasn't a good idea.'

'No? Why not?'

She presses her lips firmly together.

After a moment she sighs. 'I went with a girl from

school,' she mutters. 'I thought I'd made an actual friend. She was wildly different from me—happily married parents, money, popular, pretty…perfect…'

'No such thing as perfect,' I mutter when she pauses too long.

'No.' She draws a big breath in. 'It was a day trip with her family. I thought it went okay. But it turned out my mother was having an affair with her father and when it came out the very next day she marched up to me at the cafeteria at school in front of everyone and said she'd only invited me because she "felt sorry for me". That I was her act of charity for the week because my clothes were ugly and I didn't belong there and everyone had been laughing at me for weeks. They all sure laughed at me then.'

I know how words can hurt and when they're thrown out in public they can hurt even more. And even if Talia rationalised this as merely retaliation from another hurt girl, it still stung. Shame still clung. I know it—I know that very particular burn.

'I was happy to leave town that time,' she adds. 'But that was the last time Ava and I did.'

'You stayed put in the next place until Ava went away to university.' I watch her. 'Why didn't you move with her then?'

She pauses. 'I wanted her to be free to focus on her study and not feel guilty about me.'

'Guilty?' I frown.

'She struggled with me working long hours for not much pay. It was better for her not to have to see that. Plus I could earn more in Queenstown—and there was a lot of work available there.'

'Enabling you to work three jobs at once.'

'Right.' She picks up the other glass of orange and takes

a deep sip before shooting me a look over the crystal rim. 'Why are we talking about me again?'

I shrug innocently. 'I'm curious.'

'Well, I'm curious about you too,' she says softly.

I don't want to push her away. Her interest in me is a pleasure—I know it's not that she wants to *pry*. It's different. Given I want to know everything about her, it's actually a kind of relief that she obviously feels the same about me. Not just curious. Not just interested. *Fascinated.*

That night when she was upset thinking I'd thrown out Lukas's rabbit she eventually explained about having no things as a kid herself. I felt pleased that she told me. That she trusted me enough to tell me something painful and personal. She's just done it again now.

And again I'm honoured. It's a precious thing.

I needed to clear my own head after last night. Feeling the wind in my hair and the freedom on the water is my favourite way of doing that. I wanted to share it with her. But now I want to share more.

'I first sailed with my grandfather,' I mutter awkwardly. 'He taught me.'

Her expression softens. 'He taught you lots of things?'

'Yeah.' I put down my glass. 'Took me up in a small plane when I was only ten.'

'Is that even legal?' She shakes her head but laughs softly. 'Sounds like you were lucky to have him. And he was lucky to have you.'

I go tense inside.

'I'm sorry he didn't give you the chance to say goodbye to him,' she adds.

I glance at her sharply. But, of course, she'd been through something similar many times—with places, other people.

'It hurts,' she says. 'Even though he was trying to protect you, it hurts.'

I can't answer.

'And he didn't give you time to prepare.'

'Yeah.' I breathe out slowly. Not for the loss. I was so isolated and then his death was such a shock. 'It *sucked*.'

I take her glass and set it on the table beside mine. She's right. Having time to prepare for tough things is important.

'Phase one is complete.' I cup her face. 'Phase two is scheduled for tonight.'

Her gaze smoulders at my touch. 'What are you talking about?'

'Your introduction to my world.' I brace.

'Oh.' She grimaces slightly. 'What's phase two?'

'One of my famous parties.' I smile.

'Tonight?' Her eyes widen.

'Anzelotti Holdings is the primary sponsor of a new staging of one of Shakespeare's plays at the King's Theatre in town.'

'Okay...' She looks unsure. 'I thought you said party?'

I suspect she's never been to the theatre before. 'Beforehand, yes.'

'Before? So it's not going to be a wildly late night?'

'No, we're talking a pre-show function at a bar down from the theatre.'

'Not a debauched party at your place?'

'No.' I'm not ready to have anyone else at home yet. 'Time limited, guest-list limited. Risk limited.'

'Top-tier control freak right there,' she mutters.

'There'll be plenty of people watching. And there might be cameras.'

'You hate those.' She wrinkles her nose. 'Are you sure I need to be there?'

Yeah, I think it's important that we get on with her introduction to life here. To my life. 'You have to meet everyone some time. You have something to wear?'

Her gaze narrows. 'I'll figure something out.'

She doesn't want to ask me for help—that damn pride of hers again. I know she has a thing about *things* and about not holding onto stuff. She doesn't want to need anything from anyone. I fight to suppress the urge to challenge her on it now.

'Party.' She huffs a breath. 'Theatre. You take me out sailing, make me all warm and relaxed and now you're trying to kill my calm?' She pouts at me.

Yeah, an experience is different. An experience is something she *can* take from me.

'Oh, I apologise.' I lean close. 'But as it happens I know another way to make you all warm and relaxed again.'

I know our physical intimacy is only going to be temporary, but I don't yet have the strength to resist the power of it.

To resist *her*.

CHAPTER TWENTY-ONE

Talia

BACK AT THE house I feed and play with Lukas. From upstairs I hear a car arrive and it's so unusual I peek out of the window to see who it is. I see Simone step out of the sleek car and I'm instantly nervous. What's she going to think of Dain having a baby with a random barista?

'I've a good mind not to speak to you at all.' Simone's reproachful voice carries up the stairwell as I slowly descend. 'I only learned about Lukas and Talia when I came to Brisbane, Dain.'

She sounds hurt.

Dain's chuckle is that charming kind. 'You know I prefer to keep a low profile.'

'But not from *me*—'

'I know,' he placates her calmly. 'But I needed some time. It's important Talia feels comfortable—I want her to be happy here.'

What I've heard should make me feel good, right? But there's something off in that statement. He's mentioned it before—that I'm to be happy. He says it to Simone so *emotionlessly* that I start to worry that what he's doing for me is simply *duty*. It's like he's ticking off a checklist of things to keep me happy—putting me in a house to die for, giving me support in caring for Lukas, enabling me to regain full physical strength and energy, providing a workspace with every appliance imaginable to continue my career, taking me on trips on the sea. And, of course, sex. Fantastic, unbeatable sex to keep me satisfied.

Is it a formula he's following? Like the amenities he ensures are present in his luxury apartment buildings. Everything is perfect down to the smallest, finest detail. And good for him, right? How can I possibly judge him for trying so hard to please me? But I'm not judging him. I'm despairing. Because I'm worried it's not actually what *he* really wants or desires. I don't want him jumping through hoops trying to make me happy. That's too much of a burden for anyone.

And the problem with that fantastic, unbeatable sex? It doesn't keep me satisfied. It only makes me want more.

I brace and take the last few steps down.

'Hi, Simone.' I make myself smile, determined to show I don't need either of them to 'make me happy'. But at the same time I can't help wanting her to like me. 'Do you want to meet Lukas?'

Surely she can't resist our sweet son.

'Oh!' She holds out her arms and I place Lukas in them.

Simone beams. I glance to see Dain's reaction but he's looking at me. A small smile plays at the corners of his mouth, grateful pride warms his eyes and I know I've done the right thing in showing her Lukas. My heart swells and I flash a conspiratorial smile back at him. His widens in response and that deeply personal fire that burns between us flares inside me.

'How gorgeous...'

I turn at Simone's comment, expecting her to be cooing over Lukas but instead she's looking from Dain to me and back again. Her smile is bigger than either of ours. She walks to Dain and he takes Lukas from her with the protective gentleness he has for his son.

Now Simone looks positively rapt. 'I'm taking Talia out for a late lunch, Dain,' she declares brightly. 'We'll be back in time for the theatre tonight.'

He stiffens. 'But—'

'Sounds lovely. Thank you, Simone,' I interrupt, because I've something I really need to do and Simone has inadvertently provided the opportunity. 'Lukas is due for a nap so—'

'So that's perfect.' Simone sweeps me out of the door before he can object again.

'Thank you for this,' I say to her a little nervously as her driver pulls smoothly away. 'I've not seen much of the city yet.'

'You haven't been out?' Her eyes narrow.

'We have, just privately.' I don't feel as if I've missed anything. I've enjoyed being wrapped up in our own perfect paradise. I don't want outside interference. Or judgement. To be honest I didn't think our seclusion was actually a deliberate strategy of Dain's, but of course it must have been—because he needs me to feel 'comfortable'.

That wedge of doubt within me widens.

I know he's intense about privacy, but maybe he doesn't really want to present me in public? Yet we're doing this theatre thing tonight. And I need to rise to the occasion.

Simone instructs the driver to take us past the city's highlights. She points out restaurants and cafés, informing me which are the best and most popular.

'I'm not going to ask you about Dain.' The older woman smiles coyly. 'I don't need to. It's obvious.'

I don't know how to interpret that and I haven't any spare emotional energy to try. I'm just glad she's not going to subject me to an interrogation. That doesn't mean I can't interrogate her though.

'Would you mind if we skip lunch and go shopping instead?' I ask. 'I don't have a suitable dress for the theatre tonight.'

Simone sparkles. 'Of course.'

She takes me to a lane lined with gorgeous boutiques. I glance through the dresses. It's a good thing I've spent so many hours serving at high-powered functions. I know the sort of style that I can get away with—even if it is only off the rack.

'Can you tell me about the guests tonight?' I ask casually.

Simone shoots me a sharp look but then smiles. As I try on a few clothes she talks me through Dain's senior management team. They all sound like highly articulate, highly educated over-achievers. Great. Nothing to feel nervous about, then.

I stand in front of the mirror and look at my reflection. The black gown hugs my waist and floats to the floor, setting off the dainty silver sandals the saleswoman encouraged me to try with it. The look is perfectly appropriate for the night ahead, though part of me wants to see Dain's reaction to the small cut-outs in the bodice.

'I'll take the dress,' I say to the assistant with a smile. My budget won't stretch to the shoes.

'Let me get the sandals,' Simone says.

I hesitate. Accepting gifts requires grace and I know from Dain that I'm not so great at that.

Simone nods. 'You'll almost be tall enough to look Dain right in the eyes.'

He's the reason she wants to help me. She's genuine and she cares for Dain and suddenly I don't have the heart to deny her.

'Thank you,' I mutter awkwardly, fighting my instinctive reaction to reject her offer. 'That's very kind.'

'I'm glad you're here, Talia,' she says as we drive back to Dain's house. 'It's a good thing.'

I leave her downstairs and hurry up to the nursery to feed Lukas. Then I shower and prepare.

Dain walks into my room just as I'm fastening the straps on the silver sandals. I straighten and try not to fidget in front of him as he looks me up and down.

'Will I do?' I can't help seeking his approval. 'Simone gifted me the shoes.'

'And you let her?' His eyebrows lift. 'Progress.'

He looks stunning in that perfectly tailored black suit. I'm desperate for the reassurance of his touch but he remains eight feet away.

'We'd better get going,' he mutters.

We don't take the little sports car he drove this morning. This time we're in a luxury sedan and there's a chauffeur to drive us.

In the back seat I can't help stealing glances at Dain. It's like the night at the gondola—he's simply breathtaking in formal attire.

He catches my eye and his own gaze ignites. He half groans, half growls. 'Come here.'

Yes.

I press against the restraint of my seat belt and kiss him desperately.

'I don't want to ruin your hair—'

I don't care and he runs his hands through it anyway.

There's such urgency in my need for him. I'll never get enough. I realise this now.

'Talia?'

I just kiss him. I just want to be close to him and pretend this perfection is real. Right now it *is* real.

He kisses me back but he's gentle and tender and I want to provoke him to more because for me this need is *unbearable*.

'Talia.' He breathes hard.

His soft words ignite me.

We're *so* close. I don't care that there's a driver. I don't care that people can see into the car. I just want him. I *need* him.

But he grabs my wrists and pulls away. 'We have to stop.' He looks at me ruefully. 'Or I could send a message saying we've both got food poisoning and turn the car round right now...'

I laugh, but honestly I'd love him to do just that. I don't want to face anyone else today. My wariness rises. Insecurity completely has its claws in me. I want us to stay in our own world. Alone and intense. Because while I can put on an almost-designer dress and fancy shoes, they're only wrappings. I know I really belong on the service side of the coffee machine, not centre stage in the society he's the star of.

I struggle to catch my breath and stare out of the window as I try. The setting sun glints against the glass-fronted high-rises of the city. I've never left New Zealand before. I had no idea Brisbane is such a big city. But I can't wholly appreciate its beauty. I'm suddenly scared. And for the first time since arriving in Brisbane, I'm cold.

The pre-theatre party is at a champagne and oyster bar. The gilt-tipped forest-green ropes discreetly inform the public that entrance to the venue is reserved for invited guests only, but there are other bars either side and they're full and noisy. The customers ensconced in them stare as the car pulls up right in front.

Dain exits first and slides his hand into mine once I've got out of the car. The contact strengthens me, stirs me, my pulse regulates to match his—albeit a touch faster than normal for us both. He pulls me closer against his side.

'Is it true you're a father, Dain?' someone calls.

Startled, I glance up. I spot a camera. Then another. Someone else calls his name. I look, but I'm aware Dain doesn't. He knows not to.

I'm shocked. I realise how galling this must be for him—he's so intensely private but his secret—Lukas—is known. And he's being forced to be seen with me. To present *me* in public. My pulse skitters but he keeps us both moving until we're inside. I desperately try to slow my breathing but it's impossible because there are people…so many beautiful people.

I blink. Swallow. Straighten.

The bar is sophisticated. Its decor features that luxurious green with discreet gold trim in sumptuous curves and heavy marble countertops. A gleaming display showcases some of the oyster, lobster and caviar they serve. Bottles of champagne line the back wall. There's ice everywhere—the diamond kind as well as frozen water providing a bed for the ocean's delicacies. I freeze on the inside. I thought I was used to billionaire bashes from my time waitressing at exclusive Queenstown venues but this is next level. While it's intimate, there's a raft of people present, each one obviously very important, very sophisticated. They're the sleek elite. But they all revere Dain. They watch him, listen close, their bodies angle towards him—seeking his attention. I see it and understand it. Mine does the same.

And he's just swept in—effortlessly stalking past the press, effortlessly commanding the entire place.

We're offered champagne in fine crystal flutes. Dain introduces me but their names and faces are a blur in less than a second. Some are politicians. Some are society mavens. Some are models—at least they look it.

The noise of chatter renders words inaudible as I surreptitiously try to take it all in and note how they're all staring not so surreptitiously at me. I feel like a lamb who's been led into a wolves' den. But that's wrong, right? I'm just overwhelmed. Surely these people are nice and I'm being silly.

He doesn't relinquish my hand and, full disclosure, I can't help clinging onto him. But I don't want to rely on Dain for my confidence. Surely I can handle this myself.

Only I'm in awe of everyone's elegance. They're exquisitely vivacious, effervescent yet refined. They glitter gracefully and it comes so naturally to them. My stomach sinks. Dain's privileged and powerful and he should have a partner who doesn't only hold her own but is an *asset* to him. I've an awful feeling I'm a liability. Any of the stunning women here would be a better partner for him than me. They're all used to this scene and they don't just handle it, they shine.

I'm suddenly grateful there's a time limit because of the play. Dain introduces me to the director of the theatre and the head of fundraising and I really try to make their names stick in my mind. Mischa and Chloe. They ooze glamorous, effortless chic. We converse about nothing very much as perfectly attired waiters offer specially curated pairings of oysters and champagne. The shellfish have been prepared in several ways. The vibe screams understated, indulgent luxury but these people don't even blink. They're not just used to such rare and expensive nibbles, they're connoisseurs of them.

After a while Dain gets collared by a man wanting a quick quiet word. From dinner with his parents, I know what that means. The guy wants money. Dain glances at me apologetically but I send him a smile of reassurance. I can do this. I don't *need* him. I only have to listen and smile, right?

I talk more to Mischa and Chloe, but Chloe's gaze follows Dain. My spine prickles and I can't help looking her over. Her dress is beautifully fitted and clearly couture, her hair and make-up sublime, she's wearing a stunning emerald pendant and her hands are beautifully manicured. My nails are neat but only because they're seen in my videos. Hers are stunning. *All* of her is stunning. She catches me staring.

'Have you been to Dain's island?' she asks with a smile that makes me shiver a little.

'Um…no. Not yet.'

What island? I didn't even know there was an island.

'It's amazing.' She nods as if she's doing me a favour in telling me this. 'You're going to love it. Dain's done such a wonderful job rebuilding the house there.'

And she knows because she's been to stay? That's… great, and all of a sudden I'm reminded of the water-skiing day. I'm the charity case again—the one who doesn't really fit in.

'You *must* get him to take you,' she adds. 'I prefer the helicopter to the jet. It's faster.'

There's a helicopter as well? I don't ask. I just feel ignorant and increasingly out of place.

Our passion in the car on the way here was an ephemeral, false assurance. I shouldn't care what any of these people think about me. Talia of a year ago wouldn't have. But now I feel so very vulnerable. He's more powerful than I imagined and I don't think I can step up to this public plate and stand beside him.

'It's best when Dain is piloting.' Chloe looks at me with a smile that doesn't reach her eyes. 'Did he fly you here from New Zealand?'

I know I'm not handling this well, but I've been around people like Chloe before. I smile and swipe out with my claws, just a little. 'We were busy in the cabin.'

Her eyebrows lift ever so slightly. 'With a crying baby?'

'Actually, Lukas slept for the whole flight.'

'I bet he's very advanced for his age,' Mischa says with a genuine smile.

'Yes,' Chloe agrees with venomous enthusiasm. 'After all, his mother is *very* clever.'

She takes another sip of champagne. Inhibitions are down and tongues are looser than they were when we first arrived and even the best manners in the world can be lost.

'You make coffee, is that right?' Chloe asks.

I try to tell myself the snobbish tinge I think I hear is probably only in my head but her gaze on me is icier than that bed for the oysters on the bar and now the thoughts in my head are even more anxious and insecure. 'Yes, how did you hear about that?'

'Dain's father said you're a waitress and wannabe influencer. You do make little videos, don't you?'

So Chloe knows Dain's father and he's disparaged me. I feel for Dain. He had to live through his parents' divorce, he doesn't need his own private life being dissected in public like this. Not by a parent. And I'm not going to make it worse.

'Yes.' I lift my chin and smile directly at her. 'I make ASMR videos of latte art. Some people find them soothing.'

'It's a fad.' Chloe shrugs. 'You'll have to pivot if you want to grow your numbers.'

I nod peaceably enough but inside my pulse is skittering out of control. Chloe's right. She's also ruthless. Most of the people here are, I realise. This is a world *so* far from mine. It's *his*—hell, he's the king of it. I'm a waitress. I can make a good coffee. But who am I to hold my own with people who literally run the world? Who are beautiful and accomplished and confident? Short answer is I can't.

But I'm stuck here. I can never run away. The permanent home I long craved for is actually a prison—a gilded cage in which I don't belong and where I'm not *really* wanted. Yes, we have chemistry but, no, that's not for ever. I'm here only because of Lukas.

Two more people join us. I can't remember either of their names. I'm a good server—I can remember the dinner orders for parties of ten or more—but there are more than eighty people in this bar and I'm off balance. I'm worried about Dain. He's actually very *private*. He's worked hard to pull his company back from the brink and overcome the destruction from his parents' interference. Being the source of gossip now must be appalling for him but he's putting on a brave front. Yet he can't control their judgement of me. The undercurrent of bitchiness cements my understanding of just how out of place I really am.

I do not belong here.

My attempt to eat the freshly shucked *au naturel* oyster from its shell is awkward. They do it in unison, like a graceful ballet.

'Aphrodisiacs, I'm sure you're aware,' Chloe says, her gaze sliding to Dain again.

'I haven't been to one of these events in ages,' the new guy says.

'Dain's been too busy to host. Now we know why.' The woman raises her glass to me. 'Off the market at last.'

'Well.' Chloe gasps sharply. 'He's not put a ring on it yet.'

The entire group stares at my unadorned fingers. My not-good-enough manicure. I'm filled with shame. My self-control drowns in it and in a flash of anger I retaliate against the rudeness. 'Then I guess there's still time for one of you to make your move.'

Normally I can maintain a cool facade in front of the most demanding, rude customers but I can't keep my cool now. This is worse than when Dain and I deliberately misled Ava. Because I'm *crushed*. The life we're presenting is *everything* I want. But it's a front and never going to be real. I'm not right for it. I don't fit. I never will. I'm not good enough for him. At the worst possible time, in front of all these avidly curious people, I realise I *do* want that ring. I want it all with him because I'm in *love* with him. And while Dain has been doing everything he can to make this work, what I truly desire is the one thing he'll never give— his heart. That's not in play. And I'll never be enough for him to want to push past the hurt of his parents' break-up.

I'm devastated. I want to run. Right now. Just as my mother would. But I can't. I'm cornered like a stray animal who's wandered into that wolves' den and I lash out.

'Truly.' I shrug as if I don't give a damn. 'Go ahead. I'm the mother of Dain's firstborn. That's all.'

Even as I say it I know it's wrong. I bite my lip—offence is the best defence and I've struck out when I shouldn't have. I have to stop myself from making this worse. For Dain. For Lukas. It takes everything to pull it back together. But I'm jealous and hurt and hopeless and I just want to hide. I force a smile as if it were a joke, but they don't smile back.

I turn, leaving them with their mouths still ajar.

I'm burning with regret, embarrassment, shame.

I *need* a coffee. I'm never going to get through the next ten minutes, let alone through the performance of an entire play.

I don't see an espresso machine at the bar and I slide through the crowd, ducking my head to find the staff door. I know my way through a kitchen and find the back exit in moments, paying zero attention to the surprise on the kitchen hand's face. The back alley isn't some dank place where rubbish bins are kept, it's festooned with fairy lights and populated with an assortment of eateries. I walk into the first one that has a coffee machine visible through the glass.

I haven't had a real coffee in so long that the hit is instant—warmth, energy, clarity. I know those people's opinions of me shouldn't matter but I care about the impact on Dain. And *his* opinion is vitally important to me. Yep, it's true. I really am in love with him.

My head pounds, blinding me as what's been brewing over the last few days crystallises. It hurts. Unbearably. I'm literally losing vision in one eye. But at the same time I really see. I really understand.

And I die inside. I never should have said that to Chloe. Certainly not in front of all those people. I couldn't last an hour before letting him down. I was overly defensive and uncontrolled. I don't have their education. I'm not engaging enough to fit. I've just made myself a laughing stock. And Dain.

He'll be annoyed, maybe even angry. But maybe that's good. Because I'm never going to be what he really *needs*.

I suddenly know what I need to do.

CHAPTER TWENTY-TWO

Dain

THE EVENING IS going better than I expected. In fact, I'm almost enjoying myself. I suspected Talia was insecure about coming. She wanted to look good—as if she ever doesn't. I was going to give her the diamond necklace I bought earlier in the week on a whim I can't explain, but when I saw her in that black gown I abandoned the plan. She needed not a thing more. Besides, I knew she'd baulk at accepting it and that she'd let Simone get her shoes is progress enough for now. She straightened up and I could only stare, my mouth gummed. I thought I could stay in control but then in the car she looked at me with that desperate desire in her eyes and I lost my head.

At first in the bar she clung to my hand as if we were facing a life-threatening situation but it soon became evident she didn't need me. I don't want her feeling as though I'm supervising her every second as if I don't trust her. I want her to be comfortable, to have fun and actually *enjoy* a party for once—not have to carry platter after platter of canapés. So I talked to that soap actor wanting investment advice for a while, only to then be immediately bailed up by a political candidate who leads me somewhere slightly more private. He drones on for way longer than I like. I've only just shaken him off when Simone hurries over.

'Where've you been?' she whispers.

'What's wrong?'

'Why aren't you glued to her side?' she hisses. 'People are talking and you left her alone to...'

'To what?' I stiffen. 'Talia's perfectly capable of taking care of herself.'

'Quite,' Simone snaps. 'A little too capable.'

I frown because that makes no sense. 'What's happened?'

'She basically told Chloe that there's nothing between you.' Simone watches me closely. 'That you're still on the market.'

I blink. 'She talked about us?'

I've said *'us'*, which immediately feels dangerous. But then I'm taken aback that Talia's publicly denied that there's an *'us'*. I shut down the outraged feeling that immediately rises. Now isn't the time to feel *anything*. My teen years of suppressing emotion in public come in handy now.

'I thought you'd figured this out,' Simone whispers urgently.

'I have,' I say crisply. 'Things are good. They're fine.'

'Fine?' Simone stares at me. 'They should be *fabulous*. You have a wonderful woman and you're—'

'Fine. It's under control.'

'It clearly isn't,' Simone mutters. 'She said that she's merely the mother of your baby. That's all. That there's still time for one of them to make their move.'

Anger swishes inside—I'm an overfilled bucket about to spill. 'Talia can say whatever she wants.'

And it was a sarcastic comment, right? But one I don't

want her to say. Not to any of these people. Not at all. Especially when she's not said anything like it to me *first*.

I visually sweep the crowded bar but can't spot her. Was this event too soon? Maybe she wasn't ready. Maybe she felt more pressure than I realised. Or maybe she's messing with me and I don't know why. I thought I had iron-clad defences and could handle this.

Are we my parents creating public drama? People will talk if you give them something to talk about. And of course there was always going to be talk about us, but she's inexplicably caused more. That she's merely the mother of my child?

Rot.

How could she say such a thing when minutes before we arrived she was pressed close, *begging* me to take her? She was barely able to control herself, supple and slick in my arms, her eyes like jewels, dazed and full of desire, uncaring that we were in the back of a moving car. I battle the urge to find her, pull her close and prove to everyone present just how much she isn't merely anything. Prove to *her* that she can't resist me.

But I can't stand a scene and we're already a scene just by being here.

I still can't see her in the bar and a suspicion chills me. Has she run away from the party? The bigger question is whether she's run away altogether. That emotion I thought I could suppress so easily? It burns and my control slips. While she *wants* me, she doesn't need me. She doesn't want to need me and I suspect she doesn't *want* to want me either.

I struggle to keep my breathing even. I thought things were going to be okay. But it seems I'm wrong and my only relief is that Lukas is too young to be aware of any of this. We need to sort this out properly before he gets any older.

As I walk through the crowd one of the barmen slips me a scrap of paper. I glance at the scrawled note.

She's feeling unwell. She's sorry. She's taken a taxi home.

She's so damned proud. So damned independent. So damned defensive. I have a love-hate relationship with those things about her. Right now it's more a hate thing.

I crumple the paper and shove it in my pocket. She thinks she's been discreet in arranging this message, instead she's given the bar staff something to gossip about as well as half the guests. But I refuse to let anyone know how irate I am.

'Talia and I won't be able to attend the play, please enjoy it without us.' I mention the pertinent 'facts' to a key group who I know will pass the information on. 'Lukas is unsettled.' I smile and act as if I'm not seething inside. 'Talia's gone ahead already but I need to be with them both.'

I ignore Simone's silent scrutiny and say nothing extra to her. I tell the bartenders to be liberal with the champagne. It might help everyone forget Talia's comment. Except I don't care about any of them or what they think any more. I just want to get out of here and home to her. I want to make sure she *has* gone home.

Fear slices through me. I need to talk to her. But I need to regain control first. Good thing there's a drive to endure. I count the seconds as my chauffeur speeds through the darkening streets but it doesn't stop my brain from racing from one horrible thought to another.

I finally arrive back at the house. It's dark. I grit my teeth and head upstairs hoping like hell she's actually here.

CHAPTER TWENTY-THREE

Talia

I'M SUPPOSED TO be sitting in some fancy theatre right now. Instead I'm pacing around my room. I can't lie still because of the pounding on one side of my head. The killer headache is my own fault. I hadn't drunk a whole real coffee in so long it really affected me. I doubled back to the bar from the café and got one of the barmen to pass a note to Dain before getting in a cab. Now I'm jittery and nauseous as hell and I can't think what to do.

But my gut knows. My gut's already made me take action.

He's inspired strong feelings within me from the first. I've been passionate, possessive, jealous—yep, a whole gamut of intensity. But now I know everything I feel boils down to the one base element. *Not* lust. It's much richer and deeper than that.

I'm in love with him.

And the longer I'm around him, the further in love I'm falling. Now I feel even more sick. I can't let myself drown. I can't want it all like this—because it's an impossibility.

I've never felt as overwhelmed in my life as I did in that champagne bar with the blinding smiles and brilliant jewels and scintillating talk of things I know nothing about. My inferiority? I've never known it like that. I'm just not on his level. And to prove it I screwed up in seconds.

The door opens. I spin around to see him step inside. The floor bottoms out on me. I've no idea how I remain standing. That sickness builds in the pit of my stomach.

'You didn't go to the play?' My mouth is so dry I croak the words.

'I had a message that you weren't feeling well.' He leans back against the door to close it.

'You still should've gone.'

He stares at me. His expression is unreadable but I sense his reproach.

'You're never going to believe that I might prioritise you,' he says grimly. 'Why didn't you tell me you weren't feeling well?'

'It's a migraine. It came on suddenly,' I mutter feebly.

'Oh? Do you know what caused it?'

Not the coffee. Not even that stupid interaction with Chloe. She was merely the catalyst for my frustration and fear flaring. But I can't entirely regret it because it forced this reckoning.

'I can't do this,' I whisper helplessly. I can't lie to him any more. Or to myself.

'Do what?' he asks silkily.

The shiver of danger emboldens me. It's good that he's angry, actually. It'll make this easier. I'm wrong for him on so many levels and I don't want him to be with me only because he's afraid I'll cut him out of Lukas's life. I could never do that.

I know he's used to that denial—of time, attention, love. So am I. We're both damaged. We've both been denied. But he's worked so hard to make this work for me. He wants to be in Lukas's life and even though he has all the money, all that power, he, like me, fears loss of control. That his family, any emotional support or connection, could be taken away at any time. That he'll be shut out. He's as insecure as I am. So he's done everything in his power to make life here perfect for me. He's pleasured me over and over and over again. And I'm devastated. Because he felt he *had* to. Not because he *loves* me. Sure, he likes sleeping with me and we even have a laugh together but at heart he's only doing what he feels he must to shore up his own defences and protect his son. I understand it completely. It's what I'd have done too. The exact same thing. Pleasing. Working so hard to keep him happy. But things have changed for me. I want the fairy tale.

But he doesn't. And if he ever did, it he ought to be with someone who's his match. Someone who fits in this world. Someone who he feels strongly enough for to reconsider his position on commitment.

He stares at me as I stay silent. 'You talked to Chloe. Did she say something that bothered you?'

I bite my lip. 'I made a flippant comment.' My stomach twists.

'Is that what you call it?'

'Maybe I was too honest with her.'

'*Honest?*' He steps towards me. 'Is that what it was? When you told her in front of everyone that you're merely Lukas's mother and that there's still time for one of them to make a move? When you publicly denied a relationship with me?'

I grip the back of a chair, even more horrified. Because put like that it sounds even worse than when it happened. I felt shamed and lost control—but it was *in front of others*, when he desperately *needs* privacy in his personal life. I've jeopardised that just by existing. I remember those people taking photos outside the bar tonight. Dain isn't going to get his minions to hunt out those pictures and have them taken down. He was presenting me because I'm Lukas's mother—even if our togetherness is only to be temporary—and I've completely undermined his effort.

I denied that we have a relationship. My heart thuds as I make myself nod in agreement. Because yes, it was honest. I *need* it to be true. I need to push him away. I need to protect him. And myself.

His gaze darkens. 'Have you forgotten that moments before arriving at that bar we'd been—?'

'Of course I haven't forgotten. That happening in that car is part of the problem.' I draw a breath, but I still feel giddy. 'I can't want you that desperately. *You* don't want that.'

He stops still. 'I don't?'

'You don't want commitment. You know our intimacy was only an interlude.'

There's another moment—a flood of silence.

'An interlude that you've decided is now over,' he says very softly.

I make myself nod again. 'We were just going to let it run, remember?'

His body goes taut. 'You'd have been happy for her to flirt with me in front of you?'

My headache pounds.

He stares right into my eyes. 'Do you really think I'd go from your arms to another woman in one evening?' He lifts his chin. 'That's what you thought I did a year ago. And apparently nothing that's happened in the last few days has done anything to change your opinion of me.'

I want to shrivel up.

'Does it mean nothing to you that I was celibate for a *year*?' he asks.

I try to shrug. 'That's normal for me—'

'But if you'd met someone else?'

'I didn't…' I whisper. But I had chances. Handsome men came through the café all the time. Both before and after I had that night with him. But I was drawn to Dain in a way I've never been drawn to any other person.

'Why are you still so willing to believe the worst of me?' he asks.

He's hurt. Really hurt. My emotions spin. I'm making everything worse. Handling this all so incredibly badly. He doesn't deserve *any* of this. He deserves so much more than I can give and the least I can offer him now is that truth. He should hear it directly from me. Because I do know how much honesty matters to him.

'Tonight was a mistake,' I mumble. 'I lost control. It isn't really *you*…'

His pupils dilate. 'I—'

'No, actually it is you,' I blurt in confusion. 'I just really need to find a way to stop liking you.'

He stares at me. He doesn't get it.

I inhale deeply but it doesn't loosen that too tight, suffocating feeling in my chest. 'I want you to be *happy*. You deserve to be happy.'

'Wow—'

'I want you to be free.'

'We have a child together, Talia.'

'Yes, but that shouldn't stop you from doing what you want. Or being with whoever you want.'

'So you thought you'd speed up the process by finding someone else for me to sleep with?'

'Cheating is a hard line for me.'

'So it will make it easier for you if I sleep with someone else, is that actually what you're saying?'

I brace inwardly. 'Better still if you married someone else. But we both know that isn't going to happen.'

His jaw drops. 'This is about the most screwed-up, irrational thing I have ever heard. And I heard some messed-up shit between my parents, Talia. I sure as hell don't need your help in finding a new sexual partner.' Yep, he's wildly angry and I don't blame him.

'I thought you got that,' he says. 'I thought we had an understanding.'

Tears prick my eyes. 'Well, we need a new one.'

'And you've already thought of it.'

'Yep.' I barely hold back my emotion. I have to get away from him now. I just have to. 'I'm going to move into the pool house.'

'Pardon?'

'It'll give us space,' I blurt, increasingly uncontrolled because my head is killing me and my heart is breaking. 'I should've gone in there in the first place. Lukas will stay in the main house if that's what you want.'

'How generous of you. You've thought all this through.' He inhales. 'You're this determined not to need me.'

'No. I'm this determined not to *love* you.'

He recoils. 'You what?'

I exhale and it all just explodes from me. 'I love you! I'm so in love with you.' I can't blame this on caffeine jitters. I promised I'd never lie to him. That I'd never hold back on the whole truth. So there's no bluffing. No attempt to pretend. There's just truth. 'And I don't want to be in love with you but it's only getting worse.'

In the next second I can't believe I told him that. So passionately. So painfully.

The horrified look on his face tells me everything. He's so gorgeous but beneath that charisma, that charming smile, there's a man who's been deeply hurt. Who doesn't feel worthy of love. Who doesn't want me to love him. Who doesn't believe me.

'You're so in love with me you're trying to enable my cheating on you?' He's bitterly sardonic. 'You're so in love with me you can barely take a thing from me?'

'I don't care about your money. I never have. I only care about you.' I see the flicker in his eyes. 'You're *more* than money. If you had none you'd still be fascinating to me.'

He shoots me a cynical look that's devastating.

'You don't believe that I'm in love with you.' It appals me to realise he doesn't feel valuable.

'Words versus actions, Talia. You have to admit you've a very weird way of showing your supposed love.'

I grit my teeth. 'I want to leave you enough space so you can live your life fully however you want to.'

'You mean so I can sleep around.'

'I mean be *free*.'

'That's what you want for yourself,' he says sharply. 'You're trying to give me what it is that *you* actually want. You want to be free of me.'

He's right. I do. Because I don't want this pain—I can't live with it now and it's only been an hour since I really realised. It's only going to grow. From the look on his face I know I'm doing the right thing. He doesn't believe that I'm in love with him or that I want what's best for him.

Maybe he thinks I'm trying to manipulate him in some way and maybe this is coming out of the blue for him, but it only reinforces that this is right. What did he think was going to happen? That we would continue to sleep together just casually? Would his interest wane and he just not want me as much any more? I can't wait around for that to happen. I know he loves Lukas and wants to be in Lukas's life. Always. And he will be.

So I lift my head and answer with raw honesty. 'Yes. I do. I want to be free of you.'

CHAPTER TWENTY-FOUR

Dain

IT'S JUST REJECTION. Pure and simple. She says one thing, does the opposite and I'm too stunned to even think. I just respond from my gut. 'You've really had enough.'

'I—'

'Fine, go, then.'

Because I don't want to hear it. I can't. I'm just…*incandescent*. I can't blink away the red mist. I can't breathe through it. I've let her in and I shouldn't have and I need her gone.

'Go. Wherever you want. I don't care. Just go now.'

She looks hurt. What, did she expect me to beg her to stay?

I don't need to be rejected again. Be told twice that I'm not who or what she wants. No, thanks.

Her eyes fill. I cannot handle tears. I step back jerkily.

'Dain…'

There is *zero* point in continuing this conversation a second longer.

'You want to be free,' I snap.

People do this. They push you away right when they shouldn't. When you think everything is finally okay. But it's never okay. Because they don't love you. That's the biggest, cruellest lie of all and for her to use that one on me is unforgivable. And I can't hold back the bitterness. I shake my head—rejection of my own. 'You *don't* love me and you never should have said that—'

'I do.' She stands tall and pale. 'But you don't believe me. Because you don't trust me.'

'Do you blame me for that?'

She lies. I know it and she knows I know it.

'I'm not lying about this,' she says softly. 'But you can't believe me because you don't feel worthy of love.'

I'm stunned to silence as she stares at me with intensity in her eyes.

In the end I can only mutter weakly, 'And you do?'

'I didn't before,' she admits huskily. 'But I do now. Now I know I should and could have it. So can you. But the thing is, you don't want that from me. And I didn't mean to make things even more awkward for you.'

Awkward. She thinks she's made things awkward. She's made everything utterly unbearable.

I walk out of the room, unable to say anything more. I walk out of the house, unable to stand anything any more. I just walk out and keep walking. I do the one thing I promised I wouldn't. I leave them.

But she's already given up on me. She's decided that this isn't going to work.

I don't like quitting. I don't like failure. But I'm so angry with her. I want to smash something. Instead I storm down the road and head to the river.

I already know relationships don't last but she's ending ours way before time. Why? Because she *loves* me?

It's laughable. The worst, cruellest joke.

I don't want to think. I can't. It's too painful. But with

every step I take away from the house her words echo in my head. She's ripped me open and poured salt onto the wounds.

My parents excelled in playing out their personal issues publicly for point-scoring in their war. They used me over and over in that way. My parents also kept the most *important* thing secret from me—together with my grandfather they kept his terminal cancer diagnosis from me.

But maybe Talia didn't mean to do that. She looked horrified when I accused her of going public and that was when she pushed me away totally. It was for *my* benefit, she argued. For my freedom.

I try to remember—try to work out where it went wrong tonight. I stood with her at the start, holding her hand. She was quiet but charming. I believed her capable. I thought I could walk away. I thought she had the security. I was completely wrong.

In that moment at the party with Chloe, Talia was trying to protect *herself*. She was wounded and she exploded. Which meant she was deep in an emotional storm—like the night she blew up at me when she thought I'd thrown out Lukas's toy rabbit.

I suspected she felt she wasn't a good enough fit for me or my lifestyle—but I thought I'd reassured her. Clearly I failed and something must've happened to upset her.

The crowd. Chloe. Maybe *me*.

Talia's always wanted to protect her sister—not wanting Ava to feel guilty that she had to work so hard to help her. I have the horrible feeling she's trying to do the same for me. Because apparently she loves me.

I suck in a scalding breath because I know she lies. But the truth is so do I. I keep my true feelings close so they can't be used against me. I don't let many people into my life on an intimate level. It's always seemed pragmatic. Really it's cowardice.

Talia used to be a coward too. She lied most to those she's closest to. To the people she doesn't want to hurt and who she doesn't want to hurt her—her sister especially. But she promised not to lie to me no matter what. She promised not to hold back any part of the truth from me either.

It hurts that she has.

But her declaration of love didn't feel like a lie. It felt like a truth *tormenting* her. Something she could no longer hold back. And it was that pain that I reacted to—as fundamentally, instinctively, emotionally as I always do. I pushed back on it. Pushed it away. *Her* away.

In Talia's world she really thought she was doing me a favour but I still can hardly make sense of it. Because if she really loved me, why would she want to walk out on me? *How* could she? Surely if she loved me she could never leave me? Because I realise now—stupidly and terrifyingly—that *I* could never leave *her.*

I stop walking and try to still my racing thoughts because I'm struggling to think straight. I can't ever seem to stop and think straight. Not about her. My rational brain is never bloody involved—only the animal brain is. The lust part. The fearful part. And it's always just pushed me to action—emotionally driven action that I can barely control. Mostly I've been compelled to reach out and touch her. To take her in my arms. I've been possessive as hell from the moment I first saw her.

I want her to be mine. Just as Lukas is mine.

I could never leave him. I love him. But she knows that latter. She understands it. But she doesn't know the first. My heart squeezes and breathing becomes really bloody difficult. Talia's never had stability. Ever. She needs it more than anyone. I thought she needed it to be tangible—the house, the workspace, the life insurance. I tried to let her know that no matter what happens she and Lukas will be okay. They'll always have everything they need. But she wants more. The stability she really craves is emotional.

Talia has long hidden her needs from the people she loves. Hid her problems from everyone as best she could. She tried to manage alone for years—as if she didn't think she had the right to openly ask for help or comfort or anything she really needs.

But that night in the gondola she didn't hide from me. She admitted her fears and she voiced her needs and I gave her what she wanted. What she needed. Which was simply myself. My time. My body. My complete attention.

I'd do it again. I always will. I will give her anything and everything she asks of me. What's mine is hers.

I am hers.

But tonight she asked and I didn't hear her. She told me she loved me but she didn't want anything else from me. Nothing else. She tried to minimise herself. She shrank in front of me because she didn't think that *I* could ever offer her the same.

That's not the Talia I want to see. Ever. I want angry Talia. Feisty Talia. Resilient Talia who does what she wants and needs to. She can't shrink. She's my whole world and I do *not* want her vanishing out of it. Ever.

I want her to say it again. I don't want her keeping anything back from me. I want her to trust me. I ache for that. But admitting that I want her. Need her. That's scary.

But she *did* things for those she loves too—she helped Ava. She protected Ava by not wanting her to worry.

What she did tonight told me so much—I just needed the space to think it through. She pre-emptively pushed me away because she thinks I don't love her. Because she thinks I'm with her only out of a sense of duty. It isn't duty. It's an undeniable ache that's assuaged only when I'm close to her. When I laugh with her. When I lie in bed with her. When I'm near her.

It's heartache. And I'm in trouble.

CHAPTER TWENTY-FIVE

Talia

I WAKE AND BLINK. I'm in a room I don't recognise. Then memory bites.

I moved my backpack to the pool house last night. I don't know if or when Dain came home. I barely slept but heard nothing. I was too busy replaying that horrific conversation. I told him I love him. He tore me to shreds.

It hurts. I wipe the tears from my eyes but they keep spilling. Endless silent tears. It's very early but I need to see Lukas. I look an embarrassing mess, but the nanny won't say anything. She's the latest of Dain's utterly discreet employees—contracted and paid a fortune to keep silent on his personal business because he doesn't trust anyone.

I warily walk through the house. It's quiet and feels ominously empty and my heart skips—what if he's taken him? Surely he wouldn't. He loves Lukas. He wants what's best for him and he knows that means both of us in our son's life. I pass my bedroom door. It's open and it's obvious I didn't sleep in there last night. The staff probably assume I was in Dain's room anyway.

But Lukas's room is empty too and I reach for the wall for support.

'The nanny's taken him for a walk,' Dain says from behind me. 'He's already had breakfast.'

I jump and turn. My pulse spikes at the sight of him. He's in jeans and a tee. Not crumpled. Effortlessly elegant as always. The only hint of any strain is the stubble on his jaw and the shadow beneath his beautiful eyes. 'Oh. Then I'll go back...'

I can't finish my sentence. I can't keep looking at him. I drop my gaze to the floor and walk, talking myself through one step at a time. I just need to get away and I'll be okay. Eventually.

'Stop.' His voice is thready. 'Stay. Please.'

And now I can't move. I'm stuck in the corridor of his gorgeous home and I can't get past him. Literally.

He exhales heavily. 'You come into my life and give me a glimpse of everything I could ever want and the next minute you're gone. You leave me. I can't stand it.'

My anger lifts. 'Last night you told me to go.'

'Last night I didn't know what I was doing.'

I shoot him a startled look.

'I wasn't thinking.' He steps towards me carefully. 'I was upset.'

I swallow. 'I'm sorry I said that to Chloe—'

'I don't give a damn about what she or anyone else thinks,' he interrupts me roughly.

'But I'm sorry I said...'

His facade cracks. 'Sorry you told me you love me?'

I'm hurt. Really hurt by his bluntness. And I want to escape—to evaporate. Anything to get away because I can't cope with the look in his eyes. I can't believe what I think I see.

He holds his hand out to me. 'Talia.'

Pressing my lips together, I shake my head and fist my hands at my sides.

'Please. This is a life-threatening situation of another sort,' he whispers. 'My world is empty as hell without you already, Talia. Take my hand and let's do this together.'

'This?'

'Do the rest of our lives.' He steps forward and wraps his hands round my cold fists.

I don't pull away. I can't. He walks backwards, his gaze not leaving mine, taking me with him. Unerringly leading me to his bedroom. I can't resist him. Tears fall from my eyes and I can't wipe them away because he still has hold of me and I need him to let me go.

He twists a little just as we enter his room and kicks the door shut. 'Talia—'

I avert my gaze from the bed. 'You don't have to say anything. It's fine. I'm fine.'

'Well, I'm not,' he says gruffly. 'And you're lying.'

'Dain—'

'I didn't listen to you last night because I couldn't face it,' he interrupts me. 'I couldn't admit—' He breaks off recalibrating himself. 'I didn't answer honestly because I was shocked and I was scared.'

'Of me?'

'Yeah. And of my feelings for you.'

I stare at him, my heart pounding. 'And what are those?'

He cocks his head as he did that night in the gondola. The smallest smile curves his mouth but there's regret in his beautiful eyes. 'You infuriate me. You're annoyingly independent and ferociously capable. Sometimes I just want you to let me help you because I *enjoy* helping you, but you don't want to rely on anyone because you were hurt and that saddens me, but I get it because I was too.'

But his smile widens as his words come stronger and faster. 'You're loyal to a fault and you'll do anything for people you love, even if it isn't in your own best interests, and that generosity melts me. Your wit makes me laugh and keeps me on my toes because you don't put up with my arrogance and entitlement. You liberated the playfulness I'd forgotten I had, and I rediscovered the joy of spontaneity and silliness. And the sex I've had with you is the best of my life. I'll never sleep with anyone else. You bring *all* the feelings out in me, Talia. I can't stop any of them, but especially not the biggest and deepest. You hold my whole heart in your beautiful, clever hands.'

He breathes more heavily and lifts our hands between us. 'You could crush it. You could end me. But…' he clears his throat '…I know you won't because you're a kind, loving person. And amazingly you love me.' His grip tightens on me. 'But you need to know I love you too, Talia,' he confesses. 'How can I not love you?'

I can't move again. It's awful to be so paralysed, so afraid, but I am. I want to believe him but it's taking its time to sink in because it's just unbelievable… I can't believe him.

'I'm not like any of those people at your party,' I whisper, unable to stop my insecurities escaping. 'They're all cultured and elegant and well educated. I don't even have formal barista qualifications, let alone a degree—'

'Neither do I.' He shrugs and then chuckles. 'My grandfather died and I skipped study and went straight to work and learned everything by experience. Same as you. We both work hard. We're both curious. We both want the best for everyone around us…'

That's true.

'I never wanted any of those people. I never wanted anyone the way I want you. And it's only you I'll ever want. The night we met, you pushed a universal override on every defence I thought I had. And you were never blinded by the superficial things that surround me in a way that's sometimes suffocating.'

'Your poor-little-rich-boy trappings?'

'Trappings is right. I was a fool. I thought my value depended on the success I made of my family company.' His smile is rueful.

'It was the one stable thing you could control.'

'Right,' he mutters. 'But the night we met you saw something else in me.'

'I thought you were a stripper,' I mumble.

His smile explodes. 'And for you I can be,' he purrs. 'Any time you want. But only ever for you.'

Warmth spreads inside and what little grip I have left on my emotion slips. 'You were gorgeous. And funny.'

'Because you bring out my playful side. Only with you can I relax. I can let go. Because I trust you.'

Those words break me.

'You're beautiful and funny and I want you to stay with me. Always. I was too afraid to admit it,' he whispers. 'But I love you, Talia. I love you totally. I don't ever want to hurt you and I know you never want to hurt me either. But we hurt each other a bit last night.'

My lungs have shrunk. I can't get enough oxygen to my brain. 'I was trying to control the ending. I thought you didn't…' I start to sob but still try to speak '…wouldn't ever…want me always. Let alone…'

'Love you,' he finishes for me, and repeats what I still can't believe. 'I love you.' He lets go of my hands at last and cups my face. 'And I can't go through another night like last night.'

I blink but the tears still fall.

'Neither of us do well with uncertainty,' he says. 'So know this. I love you and I will never leave you. We're always going to be together.'

I finally smile even though I'm crying more than before and he pulls me into a hug and it's everything I need. I feel the emotion overwhelming him too—his breathing shudders and his body quakes with the intensity of relief. I clutch him and bury my face in his chest.

'I just want us to be together,' he mutters. 'Our little family. And it can be what we make it, right?'

I nod eagerly.

'I think we were doing pretty well with it, actually,' he says almost shyly. 'Not like my parents. Not like yours either. We're different people. I know I need to open up more.'

'It's hard to open up,' I mumble.

'It is. But it's also not. I like talking to you, Talia. I like trusting you. And I'm so grateful for Lukas. He's our miracle and I give thanks for him every day, especially now. He's helped speed everything up.'

I can't help my smile. 'You want to speed up now?'

'No.' He smiles back. 'I want to go very, very slow.'

Slow is torture. Slow is bliss. Slow is absolutely everything I need.

He kisses me with such reverence that I start to shake. 'Dain…'

'Shh. Let me love you. I want to love you.'

I understand. As impossible as it ought to be, this is even more melting than the indulgence he's given me before because this time the underpinning emotion is given full and free expression. His hands sweep over me and I feel him tremble with restraint.

'I love you, Talia.'

He's opened up and it's heaven. My bruised heart bursts open too and then it just grows like an unstoppable wave made of wonder and warmth and joy. I hold him—half crying, half laughing—admitting all my deep-held, deep-hidden truths too—all the things I adore about him. All the ways he pleases me. I hold nothing back. We're aligned in absolute honesty. It's always been fun, always joyous between us. But there's an essential facet that's been revealed—a foundation firmly cemented between us, within us. I believe in him and he believes in me. And it is *awesome*. I'm shaking and breathless and when he finally, fully claims his place inside me we both moan. It's exquisite and it's everything. We're together, as close as any two people can be.

'There's a lot to be said for slow.' I sigh as the gorgeous sensations stream through me.

He looks at me with nothing but love in his eyes. 'There's even more to be said for always.'

CHAPTER TWENTY-SIX

One year later
Talia

'WHAT IF WE made another movie?'

Startled, I glance up at Dain and feel my skin heating. 'Are you serious?' I squeak.

We still have that movie we inadvertently made in the pool house that time and, yep, we might've watched it together a few more times in the last year. It's always fire. Always.

'Absolutely,' he says, not taking his gaze from me.

'Now?' I glance out of the window and see Lukas and the nanny making castles in the sandpit Dain had installed a while back.

'Well, you might want a little time to get your outfit sorted first.'

'Outfit?' I'm a little stunned but *definitely* intrigued. 'You want to dress up?'

'Oh, yeah, definitely.' His eyes smoulder as he stares at me. 'I'd love to see you in a—'

'Don't you dare say maid's outfit.' But my mouth has gone dry because I'm down a rabbit hole of exciting outfits I'd quite like to see Dain in.

He chuckles and steps close. 'I was thinking more the sort of movie we can share with others,' he whispers. 'Bore them with, actually. But we can make another later if you like.'

I frown, confused and totally distracted by how close he suddenly is. 'You want other people in our personal movie?'

'Ava would like to be involved, I'm sure.' He brushes back a strand of hair from my face and his tenderness muddles my mind even more. 'Lukas will definitely need to be there.'

'What?' I'm hopelessly confused, and the way Dain's laughing isn't helping. But I can't resist leaning closer because I want to kiss him. The light in his gaze morphs into tenderness and he suddenly drops to one knee before me.

I stare and it slowly dawns. Is the movie he's talking about making a *wedding* film?

'Dain?' I'm so breathless I feel as though I'm about to faint. But I see the sudden vulnerability in his eyes and realise the full importance of this moment. 'You don't have to...' I whisper. 'We don't have to...'

He doesn't believe in marriage and I get why. He suffered so much in his parents' divorce. We don't need it. I have faith in him—in us—regardless. I know we'll be together always. 'I know—'

He puts his finger over my lips. 'I love you. I want to commit to you and promise that I'll be here for you always. I want to share my life, my bed, everything I am and have with you as my wife.' He breathes in. 'Will you please marry me?'

I stare at him and my eyes prickle with tears. There's no camera here now but it's so intimate and special the memory will be seared on my heart.

'I want to take that leap of faith with you,' he adds. 'Not for anyone else. Just for ourselves.'

He believes in me. In *us*. And there's only one answer I can give. 'Oh, *yes*!'

His smile explodes. So does my heart. He pulls me to the floor with him and we're a tangle of limbs and heat until he traps me beneath him and suddenly pauses.

'I haven't got you a ring yet… I wanted you to help choose. But I have something for now.' He pulls something from his pocket. 'I know you think things don't last, but these are diamonds. And they will.'

I gasp at the gleaming rope of jewels he dangles above me. Given their size and number I'd have thought they were fake, but this is Dain so I know they're not. 'Dain—'

'I got it so long ago,' he mutters with a gruff laugh. 'I wanted to give it to you the night of that play we never saw, but I knew you had a thing about things.'

'A what?'

He looks at me ruefully. 'I figured you'd think I was trying to buy your favour or something.'

Back then maybe I would have thought he was trying to buy my favour. But now I know better. Because I want to do things for him and give things to him. Every*thing*. And I know he wants to do the same for me. I understand his motivation and I believe in him wholly.

'The *"or something"* is that you love me.' I take the jewels from him. 'Just as I love you.'

I drape the heavy diamond choker across my throat. 'Fasten it for me?'

But he fumbles. Swears. Abandons the attempt and lets the treasure slip to the floor beside us.

Because he devours me. Because *I'm* his treasure. Just as he's mine. We're everything and all to each other.

For ever.

* * * * *

HARLEQUIN
Reader Service

Enjoyed your book?

Try the perfect subscription for Romance readers and get more great books like this delivered right to your door.

See why over 10+ million readers have tried Harlequin Reader Service.

Start with a Free Welcome Collection with free books and a gift—valued over $20.

Choose any series in print or ebook.
See website for details and order today:

TryReaderService.com/subscriptions